THE SAVIOR

Angels and Demons - Book Six

SKYLAR WEST

Published by Eclipse Press

An Imprint of
ABCD Graphics and Design, Inc.
A Virginia Corporation
977 Seminole Trail #233
Charlottesville, VA 22901

Skylar West
The Savior

Print ISBN: 978-1-63954-107-2
v1

Chapter 1

Isabelle/Sandalphon

The sun beat down from above, filling me with a warmth that had been missed while living in Scotland the last year and a half. Africa... one could arguably say, was the most primal place on Earth. The sounds and the smells of the Congo put a smile on my face. I closed my eyes and opened my senses to my surroundings.

The gentle breeze caressed my heated skin, sending a cascade of sensation through to my core. Inviting the wind to play, a particularly aggressive gust swept over me, causing my nipples to pebble. As suddenly as it came, it receded and left me in the sun's embrace. The corners of my lips lifted into a lazy smile. Even the wind liked to take the upper hand with me. Riding on that idea came the question, is the wind masculine like fire? The elements could be identified by masculine and feminine, and I liked thinking about what forces were at work and why.

A new fragrance in the courtyard caught my attention. Desiring to know its source, I opened my eyes, intending to find it. Instead, a screech let loose from my throat. Opening my eyes, there was a bonobo monkey only inches from me and perched at eye level. His stare was a blend of interest and hunger.

"Darnel," I scolded, "you almost gave me a heart attack. If you want a fig that badly, go inside and ask Gildas." The bonobo made a series of sounds that sounded exactly like he was telling me off. Then he jumped into my arms, reached inside the pocket of my shorts and pulled out a carefully wrapped fig.

Once it was in his mouth, he regarded me while he chewed. "You know, when we first met, I couldn't understand a word you said." The monkey remained silent and continued to regard me with wide eyes. I talked to Darnel like I would with a cat, glad of no hidden cameras that would capture the crazy lady who spoke to monkeys.

"As my powers evolved and grew, so did my ability to comprehend language. Not languages, but language, understanding the elements, the animals, the sounds of this world, and the others I could traverse the world above and the one where my feet are planted with a knowing that comes from a higher source. Not mortal Isabelle, but Archangel Sandalphon, whose soul I housed, provided me with an inherent understanding of existence."

Darnel said nothing, but the cheeky monkey smiled. "Yes," I cooed, "you understand me perfectly, don't you?" I talked like he was a baby. "I needed to, in order to counter that big nasty demon dragon, didn't I? Yes, I did," I continued. Darnel suddenly looked bored and rolled his eyes, like fighting a demon dragon was an everyday event. Narrowing my eyes at the monkey, I said, "I understand you perfectly. So next time you tell me to go blow your uncle, I will eat the fig, and Iver will make a hat out of you. Got it?" Darnel looked alarmed and scampered out of my arms and back to the safety of the low-hanging branch.

No longer able to contain the mirth, a geyser of laughter erupted from me. Darnel, who was now hanging upside down, narrowed his eyes at me. My laughter must have been infectious because Darnel finally gave in and let loose his laugh, which was a cacophony of small grunts and puffs of air.

"Dare I ask?" Iver's low, sexy growl came from behind me.

Darnel scampered a little higher. My threat regarding Iver most likely responsible, although the two had never been particularly close. Darnel liked mellow energies, which Iver was not, but was perfectly paired as a companion for Enoch, Iver's father. I straightened and wiped the excess tears from my eyes.

"You can ask, but I'm afraid it's a private joke." Iver pulled me in tight. His body heat added to that of the sun enveloped me in a cocoon of warmth. "Where are the babies?" I murmured into his chest. Already falling under the spell of Iver's scent, I was hoping he'd say they were busy for the rest of the day so we could have some alone time.

"The children are with my father and Sheila, don't fret. We have a moment, more and I wondered if you wanted to take a ride. I have something to show you."

Yes, my inner goddess squealed in excitement. "Well," I husked, "if it involves privacy and a secret hole that needs exploring, I'm all in."

Iver gripped my ass with a sudden ferocity that took my breath away. My nipples hardened against his chest when he slid a finger under the cuff of my khaki shorts. His finger was like a heat-seeking missile, finding my wet entrance with little difficulty.

My breath hitched as he continued to play. I expressed my growing need with a series of little grunts and moans designed to encourage him to ramp his teasing to another level. Instead, Iver chuckled. "Aren't you a needy goddess today?"

I grabbed his lip with my teeth and gazed into his eyes. He stared back at me, his hooded ice chips glittering in the afternoon light. The energy shifted and enclosed us, everything receding until all that existed was us. The seconds passed as I clung to his lip, and when I released it, I watched in fascination as he licked away the droplet of blood that was left behind from my aggressive treatment.

Iver's eyes went from glittering blue pools to something dark and primal. I had awakened his wolf, and now I was in trouble. A deep growl rose from his throat, scattering the birds from the trees. We watched as they flew hard to be as far away from the new predator as fast as possible.

Iver grabbed a fistful of hair at the nape of my neck. Like the feral hold of a wolf and his mate, he held me still. His eyes were now so dark and his package so hard that I knew rough sex wasn't far off.

Licking my lips in anticipation, I kept my eyes lowered as any she-wolf would. Then, unexpectedly, Iver scooped me up and carried me to the Jeep. Without saying a word, he put me in the passenger seat and did what he had always done, buckled me in. Leaning in, he claimed my mouth, our tongues danced, and then his teeth grabbed my lip. His dark eyes told me the wolf was in control. Leaving me a shaking wanton mess in the passenger seat, Iver jumped into the driver's seat, and we left the safety of the compound.

Not wishing to break the magic that surrounded us, neither spoke during the ride. While Iver drove, my gaze was set on the wonderment of the Congo. With no roof above us, we could see to the very tops of the Entandrophragma trees, which stood higher than the rest of the jungle canopy at almost three hundred feet.

In pockets where the sun pushed through the canopy,

motes of energy danced in the light. It was here that one could believe in fairies and magical creatures, and the farther in Iver drove, the more believable those thoughts rang for me.

Iver stopped about half an hour later, "We need to walk in the rest of the way. The forest is too dense to use the Jeep. Just follow me." And before I could speak, he was gone, pushing through the broad, dense, broadleaf plants of the jungle floor.

Iver's broad, muscular body cut a path for me. Otherwise, being in shorts, I may have been cut dozens of times. Being immortal, this wouldn't affect me for long, and an infection certainly couldn't kill me, but unnecessary pain wasn't part of my MO.

I began to question the sanity of our mission when we came upon a wall that seemed to rise for miles. "Iver, where are we?" The sound of my voice in the jungle echoed painfully loud after our shared silence.

There was a pause in nature, as if the very fabric of the earth was waiting to hear what I would say next. This aware-ness of the natural world had come upon me with the knowl-edge that my voice could manipulate the thoughts and movements of others. That was why I had fought the demon dragon, Leviathan, at the side of my immortal family. Only my gift could keep their weapons in their hands and the fight in motion. They could have been manipulated to put their weapons down, or worse, turn on each other.

I broke the hushed silence, "Appear before me, the entrance that I seek."

Iver growled as the foliage parted and revealed a waterfall, behind which an outline of a cave could be seen. "You little cheat." He laughed. "I will pay you back for taking control of my surprise."

"Then I guess we both get what we want." I moved my green eyes to peer into his dark ones. I could see the wolf and knew he wanted out. "Take me, *úlfr*."

Iver's gaze turned feral, his voice deepened when he said, "Bow." The command was clear, and that was one of Iver's superpowers, his ability to command. It only worked on humans, but any person, mortal or not, would be foolish not to obey his wolf when it showed itself.

Moving to my knees in the dirt and dropping my gaze in obedience, I waited.

"Crawl," Iver commanded. I was surprised. In the few years we'd been together, that had been an infrequent request and never outside. This part of the trek now consisted of soft sand, making the crawl easy. I made sure to wag my ass at him as I moved, thankful we had no witnesses.

When my knees reached the end of the sandy bank, and only the glittering water lay before us, he bade me stop. "Drink." His one-worded commands in his deep growl had a profound effect on my insides. Every time he uttered one, I felt the heat rise from my core and wondered if he could see how wet I was.

I lapped at the water, wondering at its purity. When Iver said, "Stop," I did. Then he was behind me, taking down my shorts.

"I see you are wet for me, little bitch." He'd never referred to me in that way before, and my body quaked in response. This was an entirely different Iver, and I liked it. He set me on edge, and the unknown of what was to come worked like an aphrodisiac on my already overloaded system.

I felt his hot breath at my entrance, and a moment later, his tongue licked me from my hardened nub to my anus. I keened with need. He pushed my chest into the sand and plunged inside me. The instant penetration sent me spiraling. I let go of my sexual frustrations from the past hour in one long roller coaster ride, not in the least concerned with keeping it quiet. Doing it in the jungle, was all the permission I needed to tap into my animalistic side.

Iver hammered into me, and I forgot everything, not caring if we were heard or witnessed by anyone or anything. The harder he pounded, the harder I pushed back, chasing a need whose surface was just beginning to get scratched.

"You are my *brúðr*, Isabelle, and I will take all of you." He pulled out and, in one motion, entered my tightly puckered bud. His hand was back at the nape of my neck and holding me still while he ravaged me. Iver had never let go like this with me before, and it was such a turn-on that I responded enthusiastically to the breach.

His hand moved from my neck and a moment later came down on my backside with a crack. His digits plundered my wetness, sending me toppling over the edge again. The heat raced up my spine and filled my chest as I unleashed a torrent. The almost bestial quality of our coupling was pushing me to feel Iver's majesty over me. I relished being taken by him.

When Iver finally tipped over the edge and into oblivion, it sent another shockwave through me, and I joined him, the exclamations from our joint rutting ringing through the jungle.

Chapter 2

Finn/Bazazath

I t had been a year and a half since I'd made my choice and stepped through the door, irrevocably changing from immortal to an immortal angel. All the fear and angst that had held me back from making a choice to ascend seemed so trivial now. The old Finn had been riddled with grief, doubt, and an unwanted empathic gift. At the time, the only way to block out all the sensations and emotions was to lose myself in gaming or painting canvases, a creative but lonely existence. A gentle knock on the door broke me out of my thoughts.

"Finn, I brought tea. Can you stop and have a break with me?"

"You're sneaky, Vi, trying to glimpse my work when you know I expressly forbid its viewing until it's finished." I could see her through the door, and it was hard not to laugh at what I saw—Violet's guilt written plainly on her face.

"You're looking at me, aren't you?" came from the other side of the door. Now I let my laughter loose.

"Yes, and you're adorable. Give me a sec, and I'll meet you in the living room, Vi." I heard her putter away, and my gaze returned to my newest work of the creature, Azalthath. My journey to his kingdom reminded me of Alice going down the rabbit hole. Neither had any idea of the new world we were about to encounter or its native creatures…

I stared at the image on my canvas, imagining that my look could summon Azalthath into my painting. Capturing him had been easy, and everything was accurate but the eyes. As I gazed at the image, I traveled back to the void, where my siblings and I had been brought after being captured by the demon beast, Leviathan.

That experience had been a life-changer. My sister, Isabelle, and my brother, Jax, had been captured, and I had dived into the gleaming lake after them. For the first time, I'd been the hero. I found Isabelle, and we landed on the shore of Azalthath's land, not knowing who or what he was. Not until a few months later, in a meeting with Cain, did I learn the identity of the king of the void we'd met.

I continued gazing into the creature's eyes and questioned what was missing? I had captured the depth that seemed as endless as the shore to his kingdom. I lost myself in the image, remembering my meeting with Cain and the story he'd shared about Azalthath and his daughter, my mother, who'd gone missing.

Pain sliced through my heart, and I imagined it was what my grandfather must have felt when his daughter had been stolen, and despite being an all-powerful god, his anger and frustration at his inability to keep her safe. That was what was missing from Azalthath's eyes, the pain, the rage, and the sorrow he must have felt at the loss of his only child. Could he be an all-seeing being who knew I was thinking about him? Had Azalthath sent the physical pain I'd just experienced, to capture his essence on canvas more profoundly?

I wanted—no, I needed—answers from the creature. Had Azalthath seen his daughter after her rescue? I made a few adjustments to the eyes, and now the creature I called Grandfather was accurately portrayed.

Sighing, I stood and stretched, leaving my brush in the cleaning solution and exiting my studio in search of my wife and the promised tea. The afternoon sunshine poured through the glass windows of our penthouse apartment with intensity. Violet had the deck doors fully opened, and the sweet scents of spring filled our apartment. The entire setting invited procreation, and I wondered if Violet had set the stage on purpose.

I grinned at the image of my pregnant wife naked and leaning back in the sunshine as I pleasured her. She was pouring the tea when I joined her on the couch. "How do you feel, my love? Is the baby kicking?" I asked her questions not because I needed the answers. I knew those already, but to carry a conversation about our bundle that would soon be gracing us. I already knew the soul that would inhabit the new life my wife was growing in her womb. But for Vi, it was all new and mysterious, as it should be for an expecting mother.

She smiled and leaned back so I could rest my hand on her belly. "Hello, little one, what are you working on in there?"

Violet giggled. "What did he say?"

"What makes you think it is *he*?"

Violet rolled her eyes. "What makes you think it isn't?"

Using my senses, I explored Violet's body, ensuring that all was well. Then I moved down to her sex. I had recently discovered that I could bring my wife to orgasm without touching her. For this late stage in the pregnancy, it was nice for her to experience pleasure without conforming to specific positions that might be uncomfortable. She told me that what I did to her was way better than those remote-controlled eggs everyone else raved about.

A wicked smile lit up my face as I sat back with my tea and, using my mind, slowly slid inside her wet entrance. Violets eyes went wide with surprise, which quickly changed to lust, evidenced by her dilating pupils and rapidity of short breaths.

"So, was this your plan, to set the stage and have me pleasure you?" Even as I asked the question, I continued to slowly pump in and out of her.

"I'll admit," she said breathlessly, "you caught me. I was hoping for some attention."

I snapped my fingers, and my wife was suddenly naked. Violet squealed in surprise. I loved seeing her naked pregnant body. She was growing a life inside her, and it made her all the sexier in my eyes. Watching the changes wrought on her petite, immortal body was fascinating, and I especially enjoyed her full breasts.

I stopped stroking her womb and gently spread her legs. "I see you are already so wet for me. How delicious." I licked the rim of my teacup, which translated to Violet's wet seam. She moaned as she leaned back on the couch. I moved my tongue inside my teacup in the same action Violet felt. She moaned loudly as she spread her legs wider of her own accord.

"I'll have to remember to call you for tea twice a day," she huffed with a gentle laugh.

I put my cup down and moved in front of her. "You know I can bring you to orgasm whenever you wish? Anytime you want, just say the word."

"Word."

"What?"

"You said just say the word, so I did." She giggled and then moaned deeply as I sunk a finger deep inside her. My morphing into a dual creature with Bazazath came with certain benefits, one of which allowed me to deliver extreme pleasure to the recipient. I could apply multiple sensations all at once without the limitation of only two hands.

I breathed air over her skin, and instantly, goosebumps appeared. I sucked on one nipple while her other was teased and tortured. Now my lovely little Violet was mewling with need as she rolled her hips suggestively.

I slowly filled her glistening entrance with my own cock, and then moving her to hands and knees, using my mind, I filled her backside with another cock. The multiple sensations overwhelmed her, and her orgasm would be one long ride with barely a pause between the ending and beginning.

"Tell me what you're feeling, Violet."

"I-I can feel you… everywhere at once. Oh god, I, Finn!"

As Violet's quivering body hit a spasming peak, her muscles tightened and gripped, sending rippling sensations down my shaft. As her jerking motions subsided to quivers, I pinched both nipples and thrust deep inside her. Again, she rode the wave, screaming my name, her powerful muscles spasming, milking my shaft exquisitely.

My eyes rolled back in my head as I added sensations to my own experience. Multiple hands now glided over my body, setting my nerves tingling. The experience could be wholly unrushed as I could pump her slowly for hours if I chose, bringing on multiple releases before finally succumbing to my own. But today was not a day for hours of sensual lovemaking with my wife.

After allowing her to spiral and drift several times, I finally gave in to my own release. My orgasm moved through me for long seconds as I filled her to capacity with my seed. When I gently released her, she sunk into the couch, completely exhausted by our escapades.

"That was the best tea I've ever had." he laughed. "Thank you for taking time away from your work."

"There is much more to life than work, even if that work is creating art."

Violet seemed thoughtful and didn't respond. Instead, she asked, "Finn, you know Isabelle and the family is in Africa. Do you think we may join them?"

"Is that what you want, Vi?"

"I want to see them. I always do." There was more she wasn't saying, and I sat patiently waiting for her to continue.

"Do you have any idea where our baby should be born or if I will have complications like Isabelle did and need help? I guess what I'm saying is I'd love to go to Africa, but not if it negatively affects our baby."

I cocked my head at her, fascinated by her line of thinking. "Are you saying that if I can guarantee you a complication-free birth, then you want to go to Africa, but if I think you may need help, then you won't go?"

Violet blushed. "Well, when you put it that way, I sound paranoid."

"Violet, I would never allow anything to happen to you. It was to save your life that I stepped into my mantle of power. But my power, such as it is, should not be the catalyst for our life decisions. After all, you won't die, the baby won't die, so what is really the issue here?"

"I don't know," she sighed, her eyes drifting to the ceiling as if it held the answers she sought. "Hormones perhaps, I just feel out of sorts here. Like New York isn't doing it for me, and I'm feeling drawn elsewhere. A force or energy is calling me, and I don't know where or what for. I wondered if we were supposed to be in Africa or Scotland for our baby's birth. Maybe something is supposed to happen somewhere else, and I'd hoped you had the feeling too and knew what it meant."

I closed my eyes and stilled myself. What used to take ages only required seconds now. I allowed myself to view the celestial world and searched for the cosmic energy that runs through existence to seek guidance to Vi's question.

At first, I saw nothing out of the ordinary. I moved through the universe as energy myself, connecting with a more significant source than what I could tap into here on Earth. The experience was tantalizing, and the wash on my nervous system was hard to describe. All I could say was when I traveled in this way, I felt renewed. Just before I was to untether my connection to the larger universe, I saw a black streak moving towards the gates of the third heaven. Inky darkness that, like the shores of the void, seemed to have no end or beginning.

My siblings and I had been mulling over the reason our rebirth into Earth-bound immortals with a required transformation back into archangels had been required of us. What was the point? Why not just tuck us away as we were or have us reborn with the knowledge of what we were? Why make us jump through torturous hoops to push for the transformation?

So far, we have had no answers. I suspected it had something to do with the war and turning the win in our favor. Iver was told by Archangel Michael to find the Savior, my sister Isabelle, and protect her. Meeting Iver led to discovering the nature of our births and the answer to what we were.

Everything happening to the immortals, especially the gatekeepers, my siblings and myself, was coming to a head soon. I knew that much. But this streak, which seemed to have intelligence, made me wonder how much longer we would have to prepare. Isabelle and Jax hadn't changed yet, and that had to happen if we were to win against the deadly dark force I saw heading towards my sister Sandalphon's gates.

I left my heights and re-entered my body. "I have seen nothing that says we must be in a specific place for our child's birth; however, being born in the Congo sounds kinda cool. What do you think?"

Violet beamed. "Yes, I think so too. When can we go?"

"How about now, today? We can pack and close up the apartment and leave after dinner."

My naked wife jumped to her feet with an energy that belied her impending due date. "I'm going to throw in some laundry and start packing for us, any requests?"

"I'm sure whatever you pack for me will be just fine. I will be in my office and will order take out for dinner, so we have fewer dishes to contend with." Violet, who was only slightly taller than me when I sat, leaned down and kissed me.

"Deep-fried prawns, please, oh, and spaghetti would be nice from Antonia's, and I'd like salad from Romeos' with garlic prawns with tzatziki and pita."

I laughed at her large order. "And where do you plan on putting it all?"

"All those orgasms made me hungry. I'll eat it all, I promise." And with that, she was gone, waddling down the hallway towards our suite.

Chapter 3

Iver

When I pulled out of my wife's perfect ass, my wolf had calmed and receded. Dropping down onto the sandy embankment, I drew her into my arms and tucked her head under my chin. "Now that we have that out of the way, it's time to see the surprise."

"There's more?" she husked sexily. "And here I thought your intention was to set your wolf loose on your unsuspecting wife."

"As fulfilling as that was," I said with a chuckle, "my intention was to show you a sacred place. You didn't think this was it, did you? I mean, this is gorgeous, and I would be surprised if any human has ever been here, as it is protected by Raphe's mother, Yemaya."

Isabelle shifted in my embrace, so her ass was now pressed into my pelvis. "Yemaya, what type of goddess is she?"

"One whose job it is to protect the sacredness of the natural world here in Africa. Her name means earth."

"Like my mother is Gaea, which is also the earth. I wonder

if there is a connection there?" Isabelle sighed, and she snuggled her warm backside into my crotch.

"Hard to say, as not a lot is known about the abyss. Is your mother, the Gaea, or another one from an alternate place? We know almost nothing regarding her origins, and we don't have a language to call your mother's people." My words set off a trigger in my wife. I felt the instant shift in her energy, and she was no longer relaxed.

"Isabelle, are you thinking about the transition?" I knew it had been bothering her that she and her former archangel soul, Sandalphon, hadn't yet melded into one. In her previous form as Sandalphon, Isabelle had been the most powerful of all. Yet now, she was the meekest of the three. Her brother Finn had evolved first. His transition had come of necessity to save Violet, his wife.

Wishing to distract her, I rolled to my feet. "Come on, lazy bones, let's get on with stage two of our journey." Once Isabelle was up and her shorts in place, we entered the lagoon. The water was a hot spring heated from the earth's interior and would be like a giant bathtub for Isabelle.

"Wow, this feels amazing. I could spend all day here." Isabelle was already immersed and looked quite content to stay where she was. It was a good thing I had come earlier to set up the cave with food, blankets, and a change of clothes. Anticipating my wife's responses was one of my superpowers and one she depended on.

In no rush to push things along, I stripped off the remainder of my clothing and joined her in the water, luxuriating in the warmth. But the best thing about this little slice of heaven was the raw energy filtering through the land. With my feet planted, tingling wound through my limbs and moved up my body, invigorating me with a deep connection to the ancientness of the place.

Isabelle had the power to levitate. I assumed an inheritance from her old soul. She rose from the water to hover several feet above the lagoon. Water rivulets ran down her skin as she gently turned, her arms wide as she embraced the very nature of the place.

Isabelle's upturned face reminded me of an enchantress, a powerful forest nymph deeply connected to the surrounding elements. As she hovered, suspended in space, a decisive rupture split the earth with a mighty crack. Isabelle dropped down and took my hands.

"Hurry, Iver, I have to get you out of the water." Isabelle grabbed my hands and started moving back towards the shore when the water beneath us opened like a great gaping maw, and a large waterspout emerged. In a herculean show of strength, she threw me as far as she could just as an enormous vaporous cloud looking like a hand reached out and grabbed her. Isabelle disappeared into the waterspout, which quickly dropped down into the depths of the water.

What just happened? I crawled a few feet to shore and reached for my shorts which held my satellite phone. Before I could call, it rang. As everything was encrypted, I didn't know who was calling, but I had a feeling it was one of the Ackle brothers.

"Iver here."

"What happened to Isabelle?" It was Finn, no doubt using angel radio to connect with his sister or her with him.

"I don't know, Finn, I was showing her a secret lagoon, and we were swimming, and a huge waterspout came up in the center. She tossed me to safety before some giant hand reached out and took her. Do you think it was Azalthath?" I hoped against all odds that her brother would know how to find her. After all, Finn was now the most powerful being existing on Earth.

"I don't know, but I'll go see if she is in the void."

"Aren't you in New York? How can you get to the void

from there?" On the other end, Finn chuckled. "Easily, as I am not there. Violet and I landed in the Congo about an hour ago. Stay where you are. I'm on my way."

I put the phone back in my pocket and got dressed. No point in contacting the cavalry if Finn could find her and bring her back. It was an odd sensation to move into waiting for stillness instead of racing to be the rescuer. That was my momentary thought. The louder, repeating litany in my head was, *why now*? We'd been accessible since the last fiasco with the demon dragon, Leviathan, in Scotland.

I felt a presence and turned my gaze skyward to see Finn flying, looking like some gigantic bird of prey. I didn't think I would ever get used to the sight. Despite my father being an angel, I'd never seen his wings. He and all the other fallen angels had their wings removed when they were booted out of Heaven.

That was another puzzle. Why take away the wings of the fallen? It didn't make any sense that only the fallen who most resembled humans had no wings, while the demon horde all had wings, which seemed like a massively unfair advantage for the opposing team.

Finn made several passes over the lagoon, giving me a salute before diving for the pool's center. With barely a splash, he disappeared. I knew seconds in an alternate universe could be hours on our side of the veil, so I made my way to the cavern where I had expected to have alone time with my wife and prayed wherever she was that she was okay.

Night fell a few hours later, and I lit the fire I had built that morning. I sat facing the entrance of the cave, watching for Finn. I closed my eyes and prayed fervently to every god and goddess for Isabelle's safe return.

Time stood still while I remained deep in prayer, that is, until I felt the presence of my mother. Slowly opening my eyes, I observed she was not alone. With her was the wolf, Vanargand. We regarded each other with identical eyes.

"Iver, we are hovering on the edge of war. Even now, dark forces are amassing around the third heaven. We cannot win unless the fallen join us with the full force of their divine selves."

"Mother, I mean no disrespect, but the fallen have never found the answers to why they were tossed down without their wings, without their power. And so far, nothing has been revealed as to how they will be restored. So respectfully, how can you ask for something that seems impossible to provide?"

My mother Freya's white-blonde hair blew in a non-existent breeze, almost as if the very fabric of where she stood was a realm beyond the one in which I sat. "You can't see what is right in front of your face, son. You found the Savior and married her, you mated with her, and your son, Arkyn, will be the greatest king in creation."

I rolled my eyes. *Did she have to speak in riddles?* "Listen to me, Mother, there are no kings on earth, at least not the type you're referring to, and the few sovereigns we have are for looks only, a figurehead without power. The world is run by independent countries that have formed their own governments. What you're saying doesn't fit the current narrative."

"Iver!" Her voice cracked liked thunder. "Listen to me. You have the answers already. You just are blind to them. Isabelle is the key, she and her two brothers, and without them, we are lost. But, without the rest of the angel force joining them, there is no hope in winning."

I scrubbed my face with my fists. "Isabelle has gone missing, taken just a short time ago, and Finn is looking for her."

She seemed not to hear me and continued her diatribe, "In four weeks, the Blood Moon will be upon us, and you must all be ready to fight. The immortals must stand together and

prevail, or this Earth that you love so much will be gone."
With the word *gone,* she vanished, and the wolf with her.

I stared at the lagoon for a long time after she left, wondering, beyond the obvious, how the three siblings were the key. My thoughts traveled back to my meeting with Finn and Cain and the story Cain shared about the trio's origins. What had been the gain in hiding the birth of the great archangels' reincarnation here on Earth?

Centouri and Gaea had made it challenging to discover what Isabelle and her brothers were. For the longest time, we assumed Isabelle had been placed in an immortal family. By protecting the daughter, the Savior, life for immortals would continue. But when we found no birth records for her brothers, we knew something was up. Eventually, Egan and my father figured it out. And the truth of it was verified by Michael when the siblings called upon him in Scotland.

Gaea had been stolen from her father, a being considered equal to the Christian God. Then someone, presumably God, extinguished his three most potent angels and had them born into immortal beings, retaining the powers bestowed on Centouri by the creature of the abyss, Gaea's father.

One would almost think that God wanted to secure a win for the future, and maybe that is why he never allowed the creature Azalthath to leave his kingdom and rescue his daughter. Perhaps he sent Centouri for his own selfish purpose? Then what, Centouri fell in love with Gaea and defied the orders he was given? Why were there no simple answers? Despite my mother's proclamation of them being right before my eyes, I highly disagreed.

Maybe *eyes* were a metaphor, like the windows to the soul. Things that reflected back were metaphors for the eyes... I continued to gaze into the lagoon and saw the moon's reflection on its glassy surface. I replayed the events that took place earlier, the waterspout spiraling up towards the sky and the great hand that emerged. Who was capable of such a feat?

Maybe whoever or whatever took Isabelle was not any of the players whose identity we already knew. Could the hand be some type of elemental energy? Isabelle didn't seem afraid, at least not for herself. I didn't like questions to which the answers were mercurial.

I sighed and stood to my feet. I used my satellite phone to call my father. The sun was rising, and my children would be waking soon to find their parents had not come home.

"Iver, any news?"

"No. Finn arrived and dove in after her, but that was hours ago. I haven't seen him or Isabelle since. If you're still okay with watching over the kids, I would like to stay here and wait."

"Of course, son, no problem at all."

"Dad, Mother visited me. She said the dark forces were gathering at the gates of Sandalphon's realm, that on the next Blood Moon, we had to be battle-ready. Maybe call Egan and look into anything that can help us figure out how to restore you and the rest of the original fallen to your celestial status. Apparently, we are destined to fail unless all twelve transition."

I felt my father's hesitation on the other end of the phone. "I don't think there are twelve fallen still alive, Iver, regardless, we only know of five we could call on. So, who are the other seven?"

It was my turn to hesitate because I knew what I was going to say sounded crazy. "I have a theory, and if I'm right, there will be twelve to fight alongside the gods. I have to go, the water is moving, and I'm hoping that what pops out is my wife, or at least an answer." I put my phone away, went to the cave entrance, and gazed out to the lagoon with a hopeful heart.

Chapter 4

Isabelle/Sandalphon

Iver's hidden spot contained so much power that I found myself drunk on the headiness from it. I was almost too late in getting him to safety when the spout opened and the vaporous hand reached for me.

I had hoped it would be my grandfather from the abyss, that he was taking me to his realm to tell me how to rescue my parents. But despite the looks of being sucked down deep into the earth's core, I spiraled somewhere I had never been before.

I wasn't afraid despite being clueless about my destination. For some reason, Finn's description of landing in Heaven and traveling down a hallway of doors plagued my thoughts as I jettisoned through time and space.

Eventually, I was brought to a castle, a mirror image of Balmorton, our castle in Scotland. It shimmered in an energy field that confirmed I was a long way from home. Approaching the front entrance, I walked up the vast stone steps and opened the door.

As I searched the main floor, there was nothing to indicate

where or why I was here. When I walked up the staircase and chanced a glance out the windows, I noticed the view was nothing but white mist, very different from the Highlands' rolling fields back home.

The second and third floors appeared as they did at home, but the rooms were empty, which I found unsettling. Knowing there was only one place left to go, I shuddered and took a breath as I made my way down, down, into the bowels of the dungeon.

Instead of a door, there was a gate. I passed through the gate, and as I did, the mist that was in abundance outside suddenly appeared, swirling around my feet and adding to the disembodied sensations I was experiencing. A long line of doors with small windows inside them appeared ahead, and as I approached, the hallway of doors extended, almost as if it was an optical illusion. The closer I got, the longer the hallway of doors became.

Stopping and peering inside the first door's window, I saw nothing at first. As I was about to turn away, a swirl moved about the room and morphed into an essence I recognized. I narrowed my eyes at the being on the opposite side of the window.

"Why are you inside this cell? Are you trapped?"

"I am, and you must let me out, Isabelle."

"You're not Jax, but you sound like him."

"I'm not Jax. He was born of my soul."

"Metatron?"

"In the flesh, or I should say in the spirit."

"I don't understand why am I here, who brought me, and why are you locked away? If Jax was born of your spirit, wouldn't you be inside him? How can you be in both places?"

"You will find many of your comrades inside these walls, Sandalphon."

I was about to ask more, but the essence turned back into

a swirl with the echo of stomping feet somewhere in this vacuous space. I moved to the next cell and saw the swirls, but no one approached me. Why would the spirits of so many angels be locked away, to what purpose? Continuing to move down the row of cells and stopping at the last door, somehow I knew who lay inside. I placed my hand on the handle, took a deep breath, and opened the door.

Inside, were two people, not souls separated from their bodies, but two people, or rather one angel and something else, whose origin was unknown to me but looked somewhat human. The two regarded me with eyes that held such sadness and despair that tears gathered and threatened to fall.

Neither of them responded, but the energy of the one who resembled a human enveloped me in desperation for freedom. I stepped closer and gazed into her eyes and saw my own, albeit with a different expression staring back at me.

"Hello, my name is Isabelle, and I think we know each other." The two tried to move but were held in position, and it was now I saw the bindings around their bodies. A rage built inside me at a rapid speed. Whoever had done this to them was a despicable, unloving being. They pointed to their throats. Clearly, their free will and their voices were also imprisoned. It was infuriating to see their utter helplessness.

"The binds that tie and the binds that hold, I demand that you let go and let go fast." I infused myself with the ability to command action. But nothing happened, and I was confused as to why, as my gift of command had never failed before.

"Isabelle."

I turned at the sound of my name and saw my brother Finn in all his divine glory, meaning that Bazazath had arrived. "How did you get here?"

He smiled. "I followed you, of course, just like the first time."

"Well, maybe you can answer a few questions... where the heck are we?"

"If I were to guess, I'd say God's in-between space, his angel storage locker."

"Seriously? Look at what he's done to them," I said, pointing to the angel and the almost human. "I tried commanding the binds to release them, but nothing happened. Finn, we have to help them."

"You can't help them, Isabelle, at least not in this form. To release the prisoners, our parents, you must transition."

I sucked in a breath. Our parents? Gazing wide-eyed at them, I saw what I'd missed the first time. While the female shared my shade of eye color, that is where our similarity ended, and hers and Finn's began. Their soft, empathetic energy was identical in vibration. The angel, he looked a lot like Jax. Running my eyes over him and genuinely seeing him, a bond formed between us. He was my father; of that, I had no doubt.

I sighed in frustration at my inability to transition, especially now when I needed to the most. Unlike Finn, there were not simply two doors to choose from. "I've been looking, but there is nothing here but these cells. How do I transition?"

Finn offered a small smile of support as he said, "That, sis, is for you to figure out. This is not my journey. It's yours. I'm here to make sure you make it back. Your husband is probably on the lookout at the cave, waiting for word that you are okay."

I thought about why I was here and who had brought me. "Finn, who brought me here? Do you have any idea who the vaporous hand belongs to?"

"There is only one I know of who is powerful enough, but that doesn't mean there aren't others equally powerful. What I don't understand is why your task is so much more complicated than my own. You are in a replica of the castle back in Scotland, and there has to be a reason for it, a clue."

I thought about the likeness. What did I learn in Balmorton that could help me here? All that came to mind was the peace that encompassed me on my two-week honeymoon. Iver and I had spent almost all of it in our suite. At the time, I was blown away by the ancient and rugged beauty of the Highlands. I felt I belonged there, and it became home... home. That was it.

"Finn, I know what I have to do. Keep watch over me, would you?"

I sat on the floor in the room where my parents were held captive. Finn hovered above me with his eyes trained on the door. "Sandalphon," I spoke, "I know you are here with me. I need you. I need you so we can go home and save our friends and family. Tell me where you are."

I sent out tendrils to all the corners of the dream castle, God's celestial prison locker as my brother had called it, and felt peace overcome me, and when I rose to my feet, I followed the path that pulled me into its embrace, home. Through the castle, I wandered, losing all track of time. I came upon a door I had missed on my first walkthrough, or maybe, it had been there all along, and I had overlooked it.

"Sandalphon?"

"I am here, Isabelle."

"Do we become one? Is that how it works?"

"Yes, you must restore your celestial power, Isabelle, and we don't have much time. Open the door."

As soon as my hand touched the handle, the door opened, and a golden light moved swiftly, filling me completely. I physically staggered under the myriad of power and images that accosted me, the speed of which was so swift that it was hard to catalog them all. The golden light I set free filled me to bursting, with the knowledge that had been removed at birth.

The passage of time, which had seemed elusive in my linear existence, made sudden sense as I became immersed in multiple timelines, life, moving in a circular pattern instead of the passage of a ticking clock.

Sandalphon now shared my body with me. "*Do not worry, Isabelle. In time, you will learn control, just like Finn has with Baza-zath. Now let us go and free our sisters and brothers.*" I couldn't have agreed more, and opening my new wings, I made my way in seconds back to where my parents' cell was located.

Finn grinned upon my return. "Thata girl."

I snapped my fingers, and the binds that held our parents dropped. What now? No one spoke, and suddenly everything felt awkward. Then those echoing footsteps permeated the halls.

"Time to go," our father said, speaking his first words. He expanded his wings, grabbed his wife, and was out the door so fast, I didn't see him move.

Finn took off, and as I followed him down the hall, all the remaining doors to the cells opened. I stopped at Metatron's. "You must get Jax to transition. He needs you. We need you."

The footsteps continued to thunder around me as the imprisoned celestial beings fled, making their escape. Finn, my parents, and I raced for the shimmering water and dove in. Whoever had opened the gateway quickly closed it, and I prayed that Metatron had made it through to Jax.

Chapter 5

Jax/Metatron

"Lil, are you almost ready?" I had been antsy all morning, and now I knew why. We'd received a call from Violet. Upon arriving in Africa, Finn had taken off to find Isabelle, who'd gone missing. I wasn't surprised. If I was honest with myself, I'd confess to being antsy for some time and knew that something was percolating. We had enjoyed peace for over a year, and I knew all the immortals used the respite to strengthen our numbers. Knowing the day would soon come when we would be tested, my gut told me that time was almost here.

"Yes, I'm ready. You said you didn't know how long we'd be, so I wanted to make sure I was prepared."

"I'll grab the bags."

"You'll be making a few trips," Lil called out. "Like I said, I didn't want to run out of clothing."

I entered our bedroom and gazed down at the twelve pieces of luggage. Lil had followed me, and I turned to her. "Are you kidding? You do realize we are going to the jungle, right? There are no corporate events, no place to wear a gown and heels. You need a week's worth of outdoorsy apparel, that's it."

"But, Jax, pleassse. I would feel naked without all my stuff." My wife was a *stuff* person, and she loved spending our money on lots of it. Our custom dual walk-in was packed to the brim with her *stuff!* I moved my closet to the second bedroom out of annoyance, a long time ago.

"Lillith, you know I love you more than air, but please, get your bags down to six. Look, I'm only taking one, and I like to dress well too."

She gazed at my suitcase suspiciously. "Okay, fine, but you owe me, Jax Ackels." There was no point in arguing with her as she would win.

Lil and I had always been on equal footing, neither of us more dominant than the other. Only when she really needed or wanted it, did we play power exchange games in the sack, and those pretty much always included my custom-made paddles for her pert behind. Lil loved being submissive in our sexual life, and it worked for us.

I went out to the living room and poured myself a glass of scotch. Iver had gotten me somewhat addicted to his top-shelf brand the first time we'd met. That seemed like forever ago now, with all the changes that had occurred since the confirmation that my siblings and I were different.

Isabelle going from a goth rocker playing drums in night-clubs to singing a bond song, getting a music career, married, and having twins. She became a billionaire overnight when she married Iver. Slowly, he'd been teaching her about business, and her first venture had been a coffee plantation in Africa. Unlike myself, Isabelle had a massive heart for causes, and her companies showcased that as she only started them in struggling economies. Iver had revived many failing economies, and our name was widely respected in every continent in the world.

Isabelle and Iver had helped Finn get his life in order after his debacle with Francessca, and everything had changed for him for the better once he moved his primary residence to Scotland.

I was still lost in thoughts of the past when Lil came in, declaring she put her formal wear and matching shoes back in the closet. "How many suitcases are you down to?"

"Uh, well, nine, but I need them," she rushed on before I could get in another word.

"Fine, but when you're ridiculed for needing extra lodging in the village for your luggage, don't say I didn't warn you." I called down to our security detail to lend me a hand, and then we were off to the airport.

I tapped my foot impatiently, wishing the trip would go faster. Lil, picking up on my stress, put a hand on my knee. "Are you okay? You seem really anxious."

"Something is wrong, I can feel it, and I can't talk to Isabelle or Finn. Our angel radio connection is not working, and that makes me very anxious. You know me, Lil, I'm the oldest, and I take care of my family, no matter how many superpowers they have."

She smiled at me lovingly. "I know, Jax; it's one of the things I adore most about you. Never having had siblings, I'm learning through your relationship with Finn and Issy. Whatever is going on, they'll be okay. No one is tougher than Isabelle, and if anyone can protect your angel brother, it's her." I smiled at that. She was right, my sister was a force, and when restored like Finn, I had no doubt she would be the strongest among us.

I was happy Iver had given us use of his Embraer Phenom 300E, which was known to be the fastest single-pilot jet in the world. We would arrive in Africa three times faster than on a commercial airline. The pilot, Ted, and the flight attendant, Susan, welcomed us like old friends. As they were part of Iver's dedicated staff, they had become wonderful friends of all the immortals who flew in our private planes.

We were about seven hours into the flight when I felt like someone was watching me. I glanced down at Lilith, who'd fallen asleep hours earlier, which wasn't surprising considering how busy we'd been at work these past few months, far more than usual. Poor Lil had agreed to a twenty-hour workweek, and it had turned into fifty of late.

My eyes traveled around the interior, and that's when I noticed the faintest swirl in the air. Chills tingled up my spine.

"Who are you, and what do you want?" I asked. My question was not out loud but in my head, for my hearing only.

"Do you not know your old self?" The image morphed into a celestial being that barely resembled a human, except the eyes. I would know those anywhere.

"Metatron?" my mind queried the being before me.

"In the spirit," he responded.

"How did you come to be here?"

"Sandalphon set me free, and now I am here to bond. You must transform, Jax. If you don't, the immortals will fail, and the celestial realms will fall."

Of course, it would, isn't that why we'd been born in the first place? To fight some war that had been destined since life as we know it was created on this planet.

"What do I need to do?"

"Get your Ax, Leviathan."

Ever since Iver told me about demons being on board his jet and taking Isabelle's necklace as a warning, I'd traveled with my ax. When Metatron melded with me, the power of the ax would be inside me, and I would be able to wield it with my mind. This was it, the moment I'd been waiting for. Finn had fought it. Isabelle was afraid of it, but not me. I had always desired it.

I sat very still and focused on relaxing, on letting go of anything but the here and now. A prickling sensation wracked my body like being hit by thousands of tiny needles. It wasn't painful, but it was definitely discomfiting.

An infinite source of information sprang into my consciousness with extreme speed, like being connected to a supercomputer. I was glad I was sitting, for the weight of this seemingly endless barrage was so very heavy. But as I witnessed the creation of our planet, the births and deaths of solar systems and planets, it was like the knowledge had lived inside me this entire time. And as I realized I had known all of this before, a weight lifted I had been unaware I was carrying. Metatron had peeled away the block that had stopped me from seeing the truth, and I felt newly born.

I saw the moment when Archangel Michael took my parents. Before leaving with them, he waved his hand over my and my siblings' heads to make us forget what our parents were and who we'd been. Then Michael looking guiltily around before waving his hand again, changing in a second the outcome of Earth and the celestial realms. We were not to forget, but instead, our memories were buried for our safety, against someone's orders. Michael had kept us safe, but why?

"Because he knew this day would come, and unlike the god he serves, he was not willing to watch everything he'd fought for and protected destroyed. Because despite the growth of the evil fallen and the deaths of the pure ones, good remains on earth, and it's worth fighting for. We can throw it back and reclaim Heaven on Earth. We three are critical to this happening. That is why he protected you against God's wishes."

"So, what now?" I asked?

"Finn and Isabelle set loose all the trapped celestial beings, myself included, and rescued your parents. Even now, they are traveling back to

Africa, and we will join them. We must unify what is left of our forces, for a new war is to begin on the Blood Moon, and we must be ready."

"Where will this one be fought, Metatron? In Heaven or on Earth?"

"It will be fought on what's left of the great plains of Africa, a fight to the death, and the victors shall inherit the Earth."

It was the prophecy, the end times, and if my calculations were correct, the Blood Moon was less than a month away.

Chapter 6

Iver

My gaze never faltered as I watched and waited for some sign that my wife was alive and well. Hours passed, as the lagoon bubbled like a witch's brew, and I fought my natural inclination to dive in and look for her. Like last time, Isabelle was lost in water, and I was not the one to bring her back. If they had gone to the abyss, I was not qualified to follow her, and it stung.

I had lived and fought for thousands of years, often with my warrior friends at my side... Raphe, Lucius, and Aquarius. He hadn't been Aquarius in almost a thousand years... Archer, he went by now. These were my tribe and the people I trusted most with my life.

Then Michael came and gave me the job of finding and protecting the Savior, Isabelle, and everything changed. The first night I saw her hiding behind Steve and Marshall, playing the drums, I felt a pull for her. I didn't know at the time if she was the chosen one, only that I felt drawn to her and wanted her in a way I hadn't ever desired a woman. I knew now it was my wolf wanting to mark my true mate. Back then, I wasn't aware of my wolf. He only showed up in dreams, and any connection was in the dream realm.

My mind was made up. I rose to my feet and walked through the cascading waterfall to the edge of the pool, where I halted and gazed thoughtfully at the water. I was not prone to hastiness. As a leader, I couldn't afford to be. Perhaps the pull was my ego demanding that only I could save her.

For thousands of years, that is precisely what I'd done. But in the past few years, my role had devolved somewhat, flat-lined. I was sharing the responsibility, and it was good, although, in some ways, it still rankled that I was no longer the best among us.

Perhaps when I melded with my mother goddess Freya, I would become something else. I tried to imagine what that would be like, but I'd been what I was for so long, it was difficult to ascertain the shifts my friends and I would go through. I wouldn't be alone in the melding with another. Diana, Albion, Archer, Lucius, and Violet would join me in the transition. At least, based on my interpretation of my mother's words, that is what would happen.

As I waded into the water, it shifted into a spout once more, and pouring out from its center, were what appeared to be spirits. Right on their heels, was an angel carrying a woman, Finn, and then Isabelle.

My jaw dropped as I watched her fly with her newly acquired wings. She was breathtaking. She landed at my feet, closed her wings, and fell into my arms. I held her tight until the hammering of her heart slowed down.

When she finally looked into my eyes, I saw more than my Isabelle. She had morphed and become what the world needed her to be, a blend of immortal and archangel, equally as powerful as Michael. "Do you love me the same?" she asked hesitantly. As if I could love her any less.

"Of course, I love you the same, and by the way, you make a super sexy winged woman."

She laughed and gently pulled herself from my arms. "I found them, Iver, my parents."

They had been standing a ways off, and by the looks of them, they had been roughly treated, unlike Isabelle and Finn, who were dual and could appear completely human, albeit immortal humans. The angel reminded me of Michael, and I wondered how he'd passed for an immortal on Earth to birth his children, and the woman resembled a human even less than he did.

I wrapped my arm around Isabelle and moved to stand in front of her parents. "You must be Centouri," I said, reaching out my hand. "Welcome to Africa. I'm Iver Eriskay, Isabelle's husband."

Centouri finally placed his burden down on her feet and reached out his hand. "It is nice to meet you, Iver. This is my wife, Gaea." When I reached out and took Gaea's hand in mine, I knew I was meeting an elder. She was filled with an energetic force that reminded me of the old gods who birthed the gods we read about in books today. She was like the titans; an ancientness ran through her veins that I couldn't fathom but recognized.

She gazed into my eyes with the same mossy green of my wife's. "Hello, Gaea, welcome back to Earth." She did not speak but regarded me with a wisdom that I imagined only rocks that had existed since the beginning of time could achieve. She saw everything and probably had seen the formation of our planet. She was indeed an ancient being and the last of her kind.

Isabelle held the genes of Mother Earth and an archangel. No wonder she was the Savior. Gaea turned wide eyes from me to my wife and Finn, her children. "You both are more beautiful than I imagined. Where is your brother? Where is Jax?"

"He has just arrived in Africa and will be waiting for us at the sanctuary, Mother," Finn responded. When Gaea graced him with a beautiful smile, the jungle sprang to life in a cacophony of welcome for their lost mother.

"Then let's go to this sanctuary. We must meet, and when we are together, we have to go see my father. He will help us plan for the war."

I could feel Isabelle's anxiety. She had a million questions, but her mother wasn't what one would expect, and Isabelle would have to be patient and allow the goddess to meet her expectations in her own way and time.

Finn and Centouri flew across the lagoon with Gaea, but Isabelle chose to swim with me. The ripples we created were symbolic of the vibrations coursing through my wife. And not just Isabelle, but I had just met my in-laws for the first time, and the fact that Isabelle's mother was the Earth goddess wasn't lost on me, igniting the question, who was the creature Azalthath?

We pulled ourselves onto the bank and sat for a moment. "I guess keeping your mother captive also kept the Earth moving in a downward spiral."

Isabelle nodded her head. "You should have seen where they were kept, Iver. It was horrible. They were in the same room but could neither touch nor talk. I can't imagine being kept from touching you when you were inches from me." Before I could ask questions, she was up and making her way to the Jeep. As I followed, I wondered if the freed goddess could provide our little band with enough hope to win the coming war.

Chapter 7

Jax/Metatron

I was astounded that only two hours had passed since my transformation, yet I felt like I'd been this person my entire life. My life up until my shift had been lived by a partial person. I would imagine it was like twins being separated at birth and reuniting in adulthood. Everything suddenly made sense, and I was no longer alone.

When we were a half-hour away from landing at Ndjili airport, I woke up Lillith. She sighed and smiled before opening her eyes. When she was back in an upright position, her eyes traveled to my face. She frowned as she continued to regard me with a look that spoke of skepticism. This would take some getting used to, and I sat very still, allowing her to roam over me. I was still me, but there were differences.

My clothing was tight and too short. I had grown when my two selves melded. I would need to borrow a few items from Iver as I was sure we were now of the same height and build. It must be an angel thing. I wondered if Iver ever transitioned into something more than he was, how much bigger would he get, and suddenly I didn't feel as large as I had a moment ago.

Lillith still had not spoken, but her eyes were wandering down my physique. Thank goodness I'd worn a t-shirt; otherwise, sleeves would have been a hindrance. That wasn't all that had grown. I felt my cock shift and harden as I gazed at my wife, who was the ultimate hot seductress. I was always well-sized, but now, Lil would need time to acclimatize to my new size, hardly a problem. I knew she would relish the challenge, the little minx.

"I guess I missed a lot while I slept. How did this happen? Did you see some doors, like your brother?" Having Metatron inside me, I could see how he was released from his prison.

"No. It was quite simple. Metatron found me, and all I had to do was hold the ax and invite him in. I'm glad you slept, as I have been processing the overwhelming changes ever since."

"You're huge," she suddenly exclaimed and then laughed.

"I am, and I hope Iver can lend me some clothing when we land 'cause the only thing that may fit now is shorts.

"You're sexy," she made another exclamation.

"Go ahead, Lil, get it all out," I said with a pretend sigh of exasperation.

"Well, I can only imagine the sex we'll have now. Oh my god, we can have sex when your wings are out. How friggin' cool is that! I'm so turned on, I want to rip your clothes off right now." I felt my angel chuckle, and I inwardly rolled my eyes at him.

"We can fly, as we were intended to. But more than that, I can do this." In my mind, I sent my cock inside her wet opening and felt her shudder. She moaned, "You have got to be kidding. This is crazy amazing."

I continued to slowly move inside her with only my thoughts. Deciding to try out multiple sensations at once, I added in clitoral stimulation, gently blowing against her hardened nub. Lillith was now gyrating and moaning, wholly lost in what I was delivering.

My naughty angel was seriously enjoying this, and then an evil thought… why not add in another hardened rod to take her over the edge. Mentally, I entered Lillith's rear end and pressed into her slowly until she was fully penetrated.

Lillith's eyes flew open at the invasion, and once she'd adjusted, her eyes narrowed and then closed as she lost herself in coital bliss. It wasn't long until she was overcome by her first orgasm, screaming out my name as she fell off the edge and into oblivion.

I wanted to keep going, to play with her for hours, but we were very close to landing, so I pulled away and allowed Lillith to calm her panting and return to reality.

"Can you do that from a distance?" she asked.

"Oh, yes, I can move inside you when I'm in my office and you're in Scotland."

"Oh my god, seriously. I can't wait to try."

I laughed at her enthusiasm. "We have forever to play any game you want, Lil."

"Do we, though?" she asked, all the lightness from a moment ago gone. "War is coming. Will we win?"

"If you asked me when we boarded the plane, I would have said yes, but that would have been Jax speaking. I understand the playing field better now, and I can see now why the transition was so important. That being said, I believe we stand a good chance. We need Iver's tactical experience, among other things, but now that the three of us are transformed, it will be easier."

"Wait, what? Isabelle transitioned?"

"Yes, and something or someone helped her to do it. I don't know who, and neither does anyone else. It was Isabelle who freed Metatron from a celestial prison. Whoever helped her do it is who we need if we're going to win."

"And we don't know who that is? How very strange."

I snorted in amusement at her word of choice, *strange*, indeed. The plane began its descent, and we buckled up. Once we landed and exited the plane, we discovered Gildas, Enoch's estate manager, waiting on the tarmac for us. He, Iver, and Enoch were the only ones who knew the way to the secret compound. No one knew that I was now tapped into angel radio and could pinpoint the location of any immortal sanctuary.

Gildas gave me an appraising look. "I see you have shifted, Master Jax. Congratulations, and welcome back to the Congo." I slapped him on the back in welcome. I'd only been here once before, but I had really liked Gildas. He was a stand-up guy.

"Thank you, Gildas, and how is Darnel?"

His eyes grew wide at the amount of luggage being removed from the jet and over to his Jeep. "Very well, sir, enjoying his time with Mrs. Isabelle."

"I'll bet," I snorted in laughter. "How is my sister?"

"Recently arrived back from an alternate realm and looking forward to seeing you and Mrs. Lillith." We secured the large bags onto the top of the Jeep and jumped in. I was anxious and wanted to try out my wings, but Metatron calmed me, explaining we had plenty of time, and right now, being at my wife's side was where I needed to be. I could see Metatron being the embodiment of the good angel who sits on your shoulder and whispers the right things to do. I didn't know how I felt about having him be a constant intrusion, but then again, that might shift as I learned more control. I would have to ask Finn how he navigated his privacy, having Bazazath inside him.

The ride to the jungle was a different experience this time around. On my first visit, I was a new immortal and in awe of all the sights and the feel of Africa. But now, I could feel its age, energy, immortality, and smallness compared to existence since the beginning of time. Africa was a heady mixture of power and fragility. Enoch couldn't have chosen a better location for his sanctuary.

When we arrived at the encampment, the whole gang was there to greet us. Isabelle and Finn eyed me with interest, and when I stepped out of the Jeep, their eyebrows rose in unison at my size. Their twin expressions were humorous. *That's right, now I'm the biggest.* They heard me and grinned.

Then on angel radio, Isabelle responded, *you may be the biggest, but I'm the most powerful.* She sniggered.

I was about to respond when Iver gripped me tightly. "Welcome, Metatron."

"Thanks, brother. I'm going to need to borrow some clothing until I can purchase more."

Iver laughed and pushed back from me. We were more eye to eye, but I was now slightly taller and much broader than he was, as Lillith mentioned.

"Raphe is here, with Diana. He will have some things for you. I think you have outgrown the rest of us." There was no jab in his comment but a simple acknowledgment of my new status.

"That may be, but we won't win the war without your tactical mind and your transition."

He looked puzzled. "How do you know about that? My father just finished telling me that he doubted my hunch, yet here you are, confirming my theory. We firstborns need to transition into the powers we inherited from the old gods, isn't that right?"

I nodded. "Yes. I don't know how that transition will occur, only that it must happen." My eyes moved to my brother and sister. "We need to find who is responsible for helping Isabelle. We need them to help us."

Iver's brow furrowed. "We don't know who or what it was

that led her to the entrapped souls. But now that they are free, it is time for you to meet your parents."

Two people joined the rest of the little group on the extensive veranda that wrapped the house. It was the woman I had seen when I was in the abyss two years ago, the woman who'd been haunting my dreams ever since, my mother. She was far more intimidating in her physical form than she had been in my memories or imagination.

I felt a powerful connection between my mother, *the* mother, Gaea. Being Metatron, the keeper of the first heaven, which was Earth, and her son. Our bond activated a power surge within me, the closer I moved towards her. The air shimmered around her as if the very fabric of life held her in its embrace.

Gaea was unlike any creature I had ever come across. When she was our mother, she was in the guise of a human. Here she was, pure goddess. Nothing was held back. I gazed at the man beside her, Centouri, my father. He was also different and had more of the alien quality I had seen when I had met Michael in Scotland. But his eyes, they were mine, and at that moment, there was no Metatron or immortals or angels. It all paled in comparison to just being a son.

A rare smile lit my face, and when he returned it, he was just my dad. I raced into his embrace, and he held me for a long time.

Chapter 8

Isabelle/Sandalphon

I barely had time to process my transition and meet my birth parents before Jax and Lil showed up. My brother had become a veritable giant on his flight over from New York.

"He's enormous," I whispered to Finn.

"That he is, and he looks like our dad."

I nodded my head sagely. Jax had more of a connection to our parents than either Finn or myself. My mother, well, she was a goddess, and I found her highly intimidating. Especially after watching her and Darnel literally speak in monkey language with each other.

She was the being who knew everything of the natural order. Where she walked, tiny flowers sprang up and trees bowed their limbs just to be closer to her. And all manner of beast had shown up to pay her homage. She was tiny, lithe, albeit with a stack on her slight frame, and her glowing presence made me uncomfortable.

Since returning from the lagoon, I had packed

Sandalphon away. Like a toy a child had grown bored with, I didn't want anything to do with my angel self. This all was way too much. Iver had been the leader of our immortal band for the past thousand years. Of us all, no one came close to his brains. He had it in spades and the experience to run the world.

Having the hierarchy here showed how mortal he was, despite being an immortal. His presence seemed dimmed somehow, and not only did that make me sad, but it angered me. We were a family with two toddlers and brothers, and we had friends. What were we now? Just a force, an army?

I hated it. Why was I chosen anyway? Why couldn't I have been left alone to just be with my husband and our little family?

You know why, Isabelle.

Seriously, Sandalphon, not now. I'm barely hanging on to my sanity as it is. If you start murmuring in my ear, I may totally lose my shit.

I heard a chuckle and then no more. Turning my attention back to the activity on the veranda, I noticed the twins had moved to Iver and were safely tucked in his arms. My heart melted at the happy sight they made. He was the best father a child could ask for. How the man managed to run his vast empire and our family was beyond me.

Being a superhuman didn't mean you were a super parent or spouse. You just had more power. I was still learning what Iver had thousands of years to figure out. Without him and the incredible stability he provided, I would suck at both. I was scared of losing him, of losing us.

His eyes found mine and held them. Somehow he knew of my fear. Not wishing my flood of encroaching tears to be witnessed, I chose that moment to sneak away from the group, make my way through the house, and out the rear exit.

I couldn't do this, be a super anything, and I couldn't handle the weight of the responsibility of being one of only three in existence. I fled to the rear of the compound and onwards to the lagoon. What had been a half an hour drive on my first visit only took me minutes. And when I arrived, what had seemed an impregnable wall now just appeared as a minor obstacle to me.

I fell in the sand at the edge of the lagoon where Iver and I had recently had wild sex, only a day or two ago. So recent, yet so much had changed already, and what I wouldn't give to just be a quaking mess being speared by his hard cock, as I was then.

I let the tears go. I couldn't get past why I'd been chosen. Didn't they know me at all? I was just Isabelle, and my immortal frame held a celestial being. I was still me. I guess I thought when the transition happened, I'd have a personality morph, like Finn. All of his insecurities vanished when he and Bazazath merged. He was a new and improved Finn. I wasn't any of that. I was the same, and I was terrified. Isabelle was far from being enough.

I lay in the warm sand and stared at the sky. It seemed bluer here in Africa than anywhere else in the world. The very nature of this place stripped away any sign of pretense, leaving me feeling open and vulnerable. In Africa, the realization of a singing career seemed so insignificant in comparison to a life well-lived.

That had inspired my first business venture, and we purchased a flailing coffee plantation in the Kivu mountains. On our first night in Africa, Enoch had served us coffee with our dessert, and it was arabica from the Kivu mountains. He'd said it had become hard to come by because the business was failing.

Not only did we purchase it, but Iver and I converted the process to environment-friendly and added an extension to the facility. The plantation now offered tours by appointment only, and we'd created two hundred new jobs. The locals were super friendly, and as Iver spoke their language, he had helped me put it all together.

Iver… he was my everything, and if this war went wrong, there was a good chance he would die. That couldn't happen, as our children needed him to be the rock of our little family. I sighed in resignation at the defeat that was rampaging through me like a disease.

I sensed the presence of my husband long before I heard him. He stood above, gazing down. "Have I not repeatedly requested that you not go beyond the compound alone? Superbeing or not, it is dangerous, Isabelle, and I don't like to repeat myself."

My lady parts squeezed at his tone. Iver's voice melted me into my most essential parts. All that mattered to me was what we shared. No amount of money or lifestyle could compete with how he made me feel. I lost it again and rolled onto my side to let the tears slide onto the sand.

Iver sat down beside me. "Isabelle, what is going on with you? I haven't seen you this messed up since your brother's engagement party."

"I'm afraid."

Iver lay beside me in the sand. He studied me as we lay face to face. I allowed myself to be bare, not bothering to hide anything from his scrutinous gaze.

"You are one of the most powerful beings in creation, Isabelle. What are you afraid of?"

How do I share my character failings with the perfect man because that was what Iver was, perfect. "Finn changed when he transformed, and all of his character flaws seemed to disappear overnight. He no longer suffers from negative energy or energy vampires, nor does he struggle with decision-making. It's like he became a superhuman slash angel overnight. I haven't changed, Iver. I'm precisely the same Isabelle I've been all along. I grew an inch, but nothing else changed. How can I be this all-powerful being when I'm riddled with doubt and fear? How can I be some fearless leader when I'm terrified to lead? I played drums for a reason, Iver, as it allowed me to hide in the back. And I'm not the leader of the immortals or our family; you are, and I like it that way. I don't want this or the responsibility. We all know I'm far from perfect. I'm so far away from being the ideal anything."

Iver's blue ice chips melted into pools of humor right before my eyes as he began to chuckle, then outright laugh, at my admission. I narrowed my eyes.

"Isabelle," he finally wheezed, "you are so precious."

My eyes narrowed a little bit more. "Do you care to share what you find so amusing, husband?"

"You are so amusing. Listen, Finn changed because he needed to. More than you and Jax, Finn was the furthest from where he needed to be, and that is why his transformation was so monumental. If anything, you should admire his ability to shed his old self and bond with his angel to become a newer version. He's like Finn 2.0."

I smiled. Finn 2.0 was amusing and so accurate.

"You, my love, are perfectly imperfect, and as such, you didn't need to change. Isabelle, your power comes from knowing who you are. Never have I doubted that, and neither does anyone else. And you have never backed down from a challenge. Finn was always looking for ways to avoid what made him uncomfortable, but you are like a chameleon and find ways to do what must be done in ways that work for you, and that, dear heart, is your power."

Inside, I could just make out Sandalphon clapping. I shut him out and turned my attention back to my husband. "So, I'm still me? And that's enough?"

Iver slid on top of me. "I told you a long time ago that no matter what happens, you belong to me, and I'm your master, not anyone else or anything else. I will lead our little family and our immortals as I always have, and you, my queen, will always be at my side."

His words pushed at my armor, and I shed my feelings from earlier. "I love you, Iver, and I need you." His mouth closed over mine, taking hold and dominating me. Beneath him, any remaining resistance melted from my body. Iver tugged down my shorts and entered me like a warrior staking his claim on a prize. I didn't try to take over or even guide the pace but simply allowed him to take me any way he wished while I succumbed to bliss beneath him.

Chapter 9

Gaea

Seeing what my children had become, was almost as overwhelming as being freed from my bonds. While it may have been only twenty-three Earth years in celestial prison time, it was a hundred and twenty-three years since I had seen them. The passage of time was made worse by the inability to move or speak.

In retrospect, it was hard to know what would have been worse, being imprisoned with the love of your life and not being able to touch or talk, or being separated with the endless torment of not knowing if your man still lived. As I didn't know the other suffering, I counted myself lucky that we were freed together.

Centouri had given up hope that rescue would come. I could see his light dim with every passing year. But I had been haunting Jax's dreams for some time and knew that our rescue was on his mind.

Imagine our surprise when our only daughter opened the door. Isabelle, the youngest of our children, managed to survive childhood without parents and a demon attack. She had grown and met Iver Eriskay. I didn't know his father, Enoch, but my mate knew of him and had been in Heaven at the same time, though they never met.

The two spoke quietly off to one side while I was surrounded by my sons and their wives. I critiqued each in turn and found the bond between them heartwarming. Isabelle had run off, with Iver hot on her heels. And who could blame her? She was shouldering a considerable burden, and she was so new to her alter ego, Sandalphon.

If she was anything like me, and I was sure she was, Isabelle would be searching for answers as to why her, and her man would be helping to navigate the answer. Iver Eriskay was quite the immortal, the most powerful I'd ever met, and his mind was equally impressive. Michael had gotten it right when he put Iver in charge of protecting Isabelle.

Michael... it was he who had kidnapped me from my father's realm and took me to be his mate. He was playing the long game too and dancing to the strings of more than one god. I didn't know why he hadn't wiped our children's minds like he said he would. Mind you, we had no idea why Centouri and I had been chosen to birth the immortals who were reincarnated from archangels and given the powers that my father had bestowed on Centouri to get me back.

"Mother, tell us what happened to you." I was drawn from my thoughts, almost startled by the sound of a voice. I was still adjusting to sound from the total silence we had endured in our prison.

"We had a preset memory inserted and thought all these years that you and our father were dead." Finn's question startled me. I liked Finn. Out of all three, he reminded me most of myself. He felt everything, the pain in the world, just as I did, and like Finn, I had done much to hide from it when it became apparent that I was no longer enough to keep Earth safe.

"My father, Azalthath, built the sanctuary between worlds for me. After creation, many millennia after the last freeze, people started to populate, and at first, their connection to Earth was inspiring. They never took more than they needed, allowing Earth's resources to replenish. Statues of me were everywhere, and every place on Earth had a version of the Earth goddess. I blessed tribes and sat among them as a human to teach them the ways of nature. As people flourished and nomadic lifestyles shifted to walled towns, the respect for the Earth was lost. With the old gods swept away by the Christian faith, so was the respect for the planet that supplies us with life. You can't eat faith after all." That was my attempt at a joke. But the little group hung intensely on my every word that there was nary a chuckle amongst them.

"It doesn't take an intelligent person to realize that the planet has been pillaged to the point of no return. The war that is coming will be complete devastation. The evil that has been gaining in the world since the fallen arrived has increased into a massive horde." I paused for dramatic effect before continuing.

"If we win, the opportunity to reset the planet will be ours. Cleaning up the mess from the last five hundred years will be our purpose. Then Earth will have time to heal and replenish. We will go back to only taking what we need. Losing this war, all hope will be forfeited, and a catalyst to the world plunged into darkness." I had not answered Finn's question but deflected to sharing what I did know. The two couples were quiet, thoughtful. Everyone in the space had hushed to hear my words and now sat in silent contemplation.

It was at this moment that Iver and Isabelle returned. She appeared restored and happy while Iver gazed at me with clever determination.

"Have you heard of the transition for the fallen, Goddess? Do you know if it is true?" Iver sat down and pulled Isabelle onto his lap.

"I have heard whisperings of such," I answered, "not just the fallen, but also the direct descendants. Your firstborns need to connect to your god or goddess lineage. I take it you have been visited by Freya and her wolf, Vanargand."

"Yes, many times since moving to Scotland and more frequently of late."

"Then you should know you and the wolf are to merge and become a powerful god. You will have the ability to transform into a huge immortal wolf with god-like powers." Iver's eyebrows rose in surprise but gave no other sign that this was news to him.

"And the others? What of Violet? Her mother was mortal." This wasn't true, but I could tell she had been fed the lie by her evil father. He wouldn't want his daughter to know that she would emerge a powerful goddess. In the battle ahead, she would help to decimate the numbers that were opposing us.

"She was no simple healer, Violet. Your mother is Gula, a healing goddess. She inhabited the mortal body of the woman who became your mother. She was only there for the inception and the carrying of you to ensure your immortality. She left then, as you are not her only spawn, and when she came back, your mortal mother was dead, and your father had turned into the evil thing he was at his death."

Violet's eyes were wide with surprise. "I have another sister? I thought Aleena was the only one." I gazed at the couples and wondered at the level of ignorance they'd been kept in. I supposed it made sense as had they been captured, they could have shared just how many firstborns there were.

My eyes landed on Iver. "You didn't really think that you

knew all the firstborns, did you? That our tribe of immortals had been reduced to a paltry dozen or two?"

My son-in-law eyed me speculatively. "No, I have never believed it, but after the attack a few years ago, many immortals came to me for sanctuary. I assumed those in hiding chose to stay as they were or were dead."

I liked this man and was glad he was with my only daughter. For, unlike the other goddesses, I had these three only. But now that Centouri and I were free, maybe we could help repopulate the earth with caretakers.

"You are correct, Iver Eriskay." My gaze swung back to Violet. "And you don't have another sister, you have a brother, Gil. You may have heard of him; his full name is Gilgamesh." That caught everyone's attention.

"When Archer and I were in the mountainous region between Russia and the coast, we heard of Gilgamesh. Aleena knows him. How ironic that your half-sister knows your half-brother, yet they are not related," Jax commented.

Violet didn't respond, probably going over the legend of Gilgamesh as being from the same region. She would know it. "There are many more in hiding, many, many more. Even now, Yemaya and Raphe are sharing the news that our fight is coming. Those in hiding must begin the journey to Africa and stand with us. There is no more hiding. We must stand together at the Blood Moon, and you, Weigand Baidya, will lead us."

Chapter 10

Finn/Bazalthath

The vacuous and watery descent to see Azalthath was not nearly as uncertain or slow as the first time. Centouri led the way, carrying his wife. Jax and I followed, and in the rear of our party, were Isabelle and Iver. Gaea had decided that her father needed to meet Iver and directly share tactical information to help our natural leader.

Our group didn't land on the shores of Azalthath's kingdom like the last time, but we flew deeper into the realm and dove into the endless waters to a domain deep below. But this was no watery kingdom. The infinite ocean had a wormhole that was air and land, and this was Azalthath's Kingdom. Considering how deep under we were, it all seemed crazy and irrational even for me.

We flew through gated doors that stood at least fifty feet tall. The loudness that had assaulted my ears on my first visit wasn't present, thankfully, and we traveled unmolested. Our journey through the giant structure brought us to the threshold of a throne, the size of which was massive, although not as gigantic as last time, and I wondered if our grandfather could shapeshift. He definitely could control his appearance, and I pondered if he had one original form.

He was approximately ten feet in height when he stood and not unlike Centouri or any of us when we were in complete angel form, slightly alien-like. Azalthath was smaller than our first encounter and challenging to describe. As an ancient being and alien in nature, he emanated power, raw energy that seemed to come from his depths rather than an elemental source. The father and the daughter were organic in design, almost as if they had been formed by the elements. It was interesting to compare us all. Centouri was an authentic angel, and like Michael, he was more alien in his appearance and mannerisms than my siblings and me.

The three of us were also divine creations, and part of us was honed from the same material as Gaea and Azalthath. Iver was something else entirely, the brightest and best the firstborns had to offer.

"Daughter, you have returned at last."

"Yes, Father, and I have brought my family, our family." The ancient being's eyes moved to each of us, and a shudder racked me as something alien probed my mind. It was Azalthath. When his eyes landed on Iver, they stayed there for a lot longer than they had with the rest of us. When he spoke, his words reverberated off the surfaces of his throne room.

"I see we have the Savior and the protector. Welcome," he said, bowing his head.

Iver, ever the gentleman, dipped his head in supplication to his wife's grandfather.

"We have things to discuss, but first, you have people wanting to welcome you home, Gaea. If you all would follow me." The veritable giant strode off his throne and to a balcony that overlooked an empire which like the sea, surrounded the entrance, and seemed to have no end or beginning.

"I really feel like Alice and I've just gone down the rabbit hole," Isabelle whispered to me. "Where is this place, like, really, where is it? Beneath the Earth's crust, maybe? Finn, remember that show we watched, Journey to the Center of the Earth? I'm just waiting for the dinosaurs to pop out."

I tried not to laugh out loud and instead cleared my throat to cover my laughter. "I thought we were in some type of middle-Earth situation, like Lord of the Rings, and when we turn our back, all the immortals will sail back to Valinor as only they can sail a straight line." Isabelle and I must have been a little more affected by our impossible situation as we couldn't stop the laughter. We sounded like crazy people, and both our parents and grandfather watched us like we were from another planet.

Jax, acting like the typical eldest, stood with his hands on his hips and sighed in exasperation, and that was all it took. Both Issy and I let loose laughing so hard, both of us had tears leaking from our eyes. If you didn't know Iver well, you would think he had no opinion regarding our childish antics. Except the constant tick that repeatedly throbbed on the left side of his jaw showed his level of annoyance. I immediately stopped laughing and took a few wheezing breaths. This seemed to calm Isabelle, who wiped away her tears and shrugged her shoulders to straighten them.

"Ah, sorry, this all is just so out of a science fiction novel. Please continue." In unison, the three gods turned and continued on their way. Jax used one hand to point two fingers at his eyes and then at us, alluding to that he was watching us.

Isabelle started chuckling again when Jax stormed off after our parents. I was about to say something sarcastic when Iver placed one hand on my shoulder and one hand on his wife's. "Not another word, you two, now march."

We followed after the group, keeping our eyes turned to the floor. Iver kept a steel grip on both of our shoulders until he felt the shock lift from us. We stopped at a veranda that reminded me once again of Lord of the Rings. The gigantic stone platform was suspended, like in the city of Gondor. Below, a great swarm of beings stood in wait. Beside me, Isabelle gasped in shock. But before we had time to process what lay beneath us or ask questions, the booming voice of Azalthath said, "Your princess has returned to us." Cheering rang so loud that we all covered our ears, except for Centouri and Gaea, who seemed impervious to the riotous blast of the crowd.

"Welcome her mate, Centouri, and their children, Metatron the ax wielder, Bazazath the demon killer, and Sandalphon, the Savior." Isabelle shot me a panicked look before we were pushed to the edge of the balcony for all to see us. A hush fell over the miles of people who were below us.

"Fly out, children, let them see you," Gaea said so quietly that I would have missed her words if I'd been using only my human hearing. Jax, the proverbial show-off, couldn't wait to strut his new wings and did a dramatic dive off the balcony and flew just over the heads of Azalthath's subjects.

Isabelle and I took hands and dove together. Her fear was palpable. She didn't like this one bit, but she had to get used to it as she was the Savior. The following words echoed behind us were so startling that we stopped and hovered to see what they meant, turning around so we could see what was happening. "And our fearless leader, Weigand Baidya."

The cheering was so loud, I thought we would tumble from the power rush. Iver, or I assumed it was Iver, as it was a giant wolf, and I mean massive, maybe fifteen feet in length with enormous wings, dove from the balcony.

I felt the shock move through Isabelle and willed her to breathe. Iver or Weigand Baidya was headed straight for us. My sister trembled beside me in complete shock. Stopping in front of us, he spoke with his voice, thank goodness. "Isabelle, get on my back." She was frozen and would have been down and lost in the crowd if I hadn't been holding her hand. I placed her gently on Weigand's back and moved away as the leader took over. Iver was a sight to behold, and the crowd was hushed to silence by his majestic appearance.

I could see his mouth moving, but his words were for Isabelle only. Finally, she folded forward, resting her head on the soft ruff of his neck, and gently took hold of some of his fur. His neck was too large to wrap her hands around, but at least she could hold on. The crowd went wild when she closed her wings and surrendered to her mate.

Iver flew at a stately pace, and I followed behind. We caught up to Jax, whose shocked expression was almost comical. I could just feel him seething inside that Iver had stolen the limelight again. I thought it was humorous that Jax thought he could outdo the age-old immortal.

We returned to the balcony and the smiles of appreciation from our mother. I couldn't wait to speak with Iver when we returned to our world and ask what had happened.

Chapter 11

Iver/ Weigand Baidya

I knew something was going to happen to me on this trip. There was no way I would have been allowed otherwise. In the oldest scrolls, there was mention of this land, the in-between and a safe haven for beings who no longer had a place on Earth so now made their home within it. I had assumed the location was not of this world but a portal to another universe. The world Azalthath had created was a monstrous feat, but I suspected he was stuck here, and I couldn't wait to find out if my theory was correct.

As I flew with Isabelle on my back, I took note of the varied creatures who lay below us and was blown away that they had managed to survive and thrive far away from the travesty being wrought on Earth by humans.

My poor Isabelle would have fallen from shock if Finn hadn't been holding her hand. When I scooped her up, I spoke to her in Gaelic, as it had a calming effect on her. I felt her shudder and relax on our way back to the stone balcony where the others waited for us. When we landed, I instantly turned back to myself, and Isabelle was safely tucked into my arms.

"I understand the importance of the discussion we must have, Azalthath, but I think we would be better served if I took Isabelle back to our realm and I came again with Gaea and Centouri to discuss the Blood Moon war."

He nodded at me and snapped his fingers. We were standing in the compound back in Africa. Isabelle had her eyes closed and hadn't opened them since she climbed onto my back and settled in. I was growing concerned with her disassociation.

"Isabelle, we are home. You can open your eyes."

A tremulous voice spoke from the depth of my shirt. "Home? Or Africa?" I wanted to chuckle, but concern for her outweighed the delight and amusement I found in almost every word she spoke.

"Isabelle, what's wrong?"

Around me, her family eyed us with concern but said nothing as they left us in peace and entered into my father's home, no doubt to talk about their shared experience of the abyss. I turned back to the wolf and flew for the lagoon and the little paradise behind the falls. When we were safely ensconced, I turned back into my immortal human form and draped Isabelle over my lap.

I slammed her backside with my hand. Squealing in shock, she attempted to cover herself. I quickly moved and captured both wrists in one of my hands. I continued to spank her while she squealed, cried, and demanded I let her go. It took a long while before she finally surrendered.

But when she did, I lifted her off my lap and laid her down on the sleeping bag. She winced when her hot, tender ass touched the hardness of the ground beneath us. She gazed up at me with red-rimmed eyes, the tip of her nose pink, and her hair falling in waves around her young face. She looked like a lost little girl. She wasn't fragile. No, Isabelle was strong mentally and physically, but I was much more so, and I used it to my advantage, allowing her to be the young woman she'd been when we met. She needed to feel safe, and I would give her that.

"Now speak to me, my little sprite, and tell me what is wrong." She sniffled and wiped her nose. I could tell she was going to make this difficult. Not usually prone to selfish bouts of drama, something on our trip had triggered her need to be a spoilt brat, and I would treat her as such.

"You will submit to me, Isabelle, and you can do it now, or there will be more consequences." I'd always had the ability to influence mortals with my will, one of the reasons for my success. But with Vanargand inside me, my command was spoken with such force that Isabelle scrambled to her knees.

"Yes, sir," she replied, bending at the waist in complete supplication. Inside me, my wolf howled his approval and desperately wanted to take her.

"Open and welcome me inside you, Isabelle." I wasn't speaking, the wolf was, and I wondered if it was a mating ceremony of sorts. Isabelle hadn't noticed yet, but I had grown and expanded somewhat with the transition, and my cock was also bigger.

Isabelle rolled onto her back and spread her knees, turning her head to the side and exposing her neck to me. It was an act of total trust, faith that I would not hurt her. The urgency to take her calmed to a steady roar within my being.

I hovered over her and then, in one swift thrust of my hips, buried myself to the hilt inside her warm, wet channel. Isabelle screeched as a powerful orgasm overtook her, and her quivering walls had a profound effect on my shaft.

My new immortality roamed through my rod, pushing my need to claim her. With this aphrodisiac, my cock grew inside her. I flipped her onto her knees and took her from behind.

Gripping her hips tightly, her red ass received a spanking from my pelvis with each thrust of my hips. Isabelle spiraled and fell off the edge repeatedly, her channel milking me hard with each spasm.

When I was finally ready to join her, a primal howl let loose, and I pumped my seed into her beautiful sheath. What felt like long minutes passed as the power coursing through me continued to pump into my mate. When I was finally spent, I released her hips, and we both collapsed onto the ground.

"Holy hell," she uttered after a few minutes, "that was crazy sex." My grin was lost on her as she was facing away from me.

"Oh, and how was it different than any other time?"

"Seriously," she said, breaking free of my arm wrapped around her and turning to face me. "If I'm not pregnant again, I'd be surprised. Your cock had an intelligence all its own and it was so primal. I feel like I was taken by a god."

I narrowed my eyes at her. "Of course, you were," I said arrogantly.

She laughed and playfully punched my arm. "You're bigger."

"I am."

"I thought your cock was going to split me in half."

"Good."

"Good?"

I laughed at her look of shock. "Well, you were being naughty, weren't you, Isabelle, and you needed a lesson in surrendering."

Her eyes dilated. She loved it when I took control of her body, even though she would rarely admit it.

"Say it."

"Pardon me, what do you mean?"

Her rapid breathing and dilated eyes told me how turned on she was. If she wanted to play this game, I would play along. "Another lesson then." I moved over quickly and placed her arms over her head. "Stay," I commanded. I was testing my new ability to control her body. She attempted to lift her arms, but they wouldn't move.

I grinned down at Isabelle and the look of surprise on her face. "That's right, my little sprite, now that you are completely at my disposal, are you sure you want to keep pretending you don't know what I mean?"

A grin lifted the corners of her sensual lips, but no answer was forthcoming.

"Arch your back, angel." She did as commanded, and when her head was dropped back, I commanded her to open her mouth. I slid my cock into her juicy mouth and down her velvety throat. Her moans sent vibrations through my cock that were highly pleasurable.

With her legs parted and her hips gyrating, I could tell my mate needed more. So pulling from her throat, I moved down her body and placed the head of my cock at the entrance of her backside. I penetrated her, slowly sinking deep inside her. Placing one of her creamy thighs on my shoulder, I took her on an angle that allowed me to also play with her hardened nub.

In seconds, Isabelle was screaming my name as she released. Deciding to test my skills further, I said, "Isabelle, no releasing." Below me, she sucked in a shocked breath. I rode her for a long time with her writhing in need beneath me. When I was ready to unleash, I said, "Isabelle, *now!*"

She let loose a primal keen and an orgasm that just kept coming. This time, I finished long before she was done. I pulled out and dropped down beside her. Minutes passed before she uttered, "Nice trick."

I laughed. It was rather fun, and it did the trick. "Now, remember, little girl, I can render you immobile anytime I wish, so you had better behave."

She grinned at me. "Or not, and get my just desserts." We both laughed at her statement.

"I feel compelled to make sure you are okay."

She rolled onto her back and stared at the top of the cavern. "Yes. I feel better now that you have transitioned. Honestly, I didn't like you being the leader. I just wanted to be with our kids, back in Scotland, swimming in our pool and having fun as a family. I know it's completely selfish, but I want forever with you, and I've been worried about you surviving this war, but now with you and Vanargand bonded, I feel a lot better. He's powerful, your wolf."

"He is very potent. Was he too much for you, Isabelle? If he was, I could banish him next time." I was nervous about her answer. She seemed utterly satiated and relaxed, but I had to hear her say the words.

"No, your wolf is perfect, Iver. You are perfect."

I sighed in relief. Weigand Baidya was not included in her glowing praise but confirmed that our experience was positive for us both. "Come on, dirty girl, we shall clean up in the lagoon, and then I think my wolf will sample you again before we return."

Isabelle smiled. Rising to her feet, she took off to the edge, screaming, "Last one in is a rotten egg," before disappearing over the edge. A moment later, a splash was heard. I chuckled and jumped in after her.

Chapter 12

Violet

O ur arrival in Africa had been far from anything I could have expected. Finn was gone before I had time to exit the Jeep. No one was at the sanctuary but Gildas and me. Apparently, the welcoming committee was looking for Isabelle or busy making last-minute arrangements at the new settlement.

After the multiple explosions had gone off around the world a few years back, Iver had taken it upon himself to help fund and build sanctuary communities whose locations were protected by Enoch. Initially, there were to be seven but ended up being four, with one right here. A golf cart drove away from Enoch's home where I was currently relaxing. I welcomed the silence of the jungle, and the cool lemonade was a perfect accompaniment to the gentle swinging of the glider on which I rested.

I tried not to think about the coming war or about the necessary transition of Isabelle and Jax. Instead, I placed one hand on my distended belly and sent loving thoughts to my unborn baby. The not-right feeling that plagued me in New York dissipated the moment we stepped off the plane. We were where we needed to be, of that I had no doubt.

I was staring at a tree, its rustling belying the lack of breeze, and wondered what secrets it held in its leafy branches, when a monkey made its appearance. I presumed it was the infamous Darnel but waited in stillness for the bonobo to approach me.

After long minutes of assessing me from afar, the bonobo ran along a thick branch that overhung the property, so now, he only sat a dozen feet away from me and could easily hop to the veranda if he chose to.

"Darnel, I presume. I am very pleased to meet you. I am Violet." He gave me no reaction. Hmm. "Darnel, have you seen the angel? That is my mate Bazazath." The bonobo glanced back into the jungle, probably in the direction that Finn had flown off to.

"Isabelle is missing. He has gone to find her." That provoked a response. From the many stories she had told me, Darnel and she were friends. His big monkey eyes grew more expansive as he chittered at me. I tried to imagine his response as, of course, I couldn't interpret his chittering. Isabelle did say he was pretty saucy and had a wicked sense of humor. How she knew that, was a mystery to me.

"I couldn't agree more, Darnel. I am quite alone and was wondering if you would keep me company until someone returns." Apparently, I was the only stupid one here because Darnel understood me perfectly. He landed on the glider with one graceful leap, sending it to higher altitudes.

Darnel let loose a chittering type of laughter that proved contagious. Taking my laughter as permission, he rocked the glider to greater heights, so high in fact, that although I didn't feel in danger, I could close my eyes and remember a childhood filled with laughter as my father swung me around.

We stayed like that for some time, enjoying the motions and the silence of our company. I must have dozed because I was startled awake with a screeching Darnel. He was agitated and was pointing to the sky. Looking up, I saw Finn flying and then something else. Behind him, was another angel carrying a person. At least from here, it looked like a human, but I noticed that the foliage changed as they flew over it. The tree-tops grew... what? I blinked several times to ensure it wasn't my imagination.

The trees reached to touch the flying couple, the sky around them seemed bluer, and the scents on the air sweet-ened. Birds flocked into the air in great groups, but in no way were they challenging their approach. Then the earth trem-bled, and I jumped off the glider, grabbing on to the nearest post.

When the trio landed before me, the pounding stopped. My breath caught as I gazed at the source of the trembling. Surrounding us were giraffes, elephants, and what must have been thousands of monkeys of multiple variations. The jungle had come to greet whoever the other angel was holding in his arms. He placed his bundle down, and the female, who was decidedly not human despite a slight resemblance, reached out her hand to me.

"Hello, Violet, I am your mother-in-law, Gaea." Holy! My eyes flew to Finn, who was regarding me with interest. "It is true, Vi, this is my mother and my father, Centouri." I was baffled about their presence and had so many questions, I didn't know where to start.

Instead, I gripped her hand firmly. We were of similar height and stature. But where I was housed in a petite, strong frame, almost boyish figure, Gaea was glowing in gold, her feet not quite touching the ground but seeming to hover just above, and her figure was more like Lillith's, entirely feminine. She was breathtaking. "I am so honored to finally meet you, Mother." I bowed my head in great respect, for I was meeting an original being.

Gaea graced me with a wide smile. "Come, child, you must not be deferential to me. We are family." As she pulled me in for a hug, I felt as if I was somehow hugging the very fabric of nature, as if she was simply an element housed in a human-like body. When she released me, she seemed to finally sense those awaiting her around the perimeter of the fence. The silence was as staggering as the shaking had been disturbing. Gaea spoke in some type of language, and the animals responded and then dispersed.

And despite the emptiness that now permeated the area, she filled it entirely with her presence. Not knowing what was expected of me—after all, this was my first time meeting a being—I offered lemonade, and they accepted. We four sat down and chatted like a family about my impending delivery. Gaea placed her hands upon me and spoke in yet another language, and the baby inside me responded with a few kicks. Gaea laughed in delight.

"You are growing a little goddess in there, Violet, what a treasure she is." I did my best guppie impersonation while the three gently laughed at my shock. "You were right, Vi," Finn said, "this is where we were meant to be."

I had no time to answer him. Enoch came driving up from one direction while Iver and Isabelle finally appeared through the gate. Time for this baby momma to find some food. I escaped into the coolness of the interior and made my way to the fridge, glad to be alone once again to process Finn's parents. I felt like Dorothy, and I knew I wasn't in Kansas anymore.

Chapter 13

Finn/Bazazath

When we arrived back from our grandfather's kingdom, Isabelle was in a state, and Iver flew off with her in his arms, probably to a secluded location to set her straight. She was overwrought and needed some time to adjust, I presumed. We turned to enter the house when I heard, "Where's my husband?" then a screech of someone in pain, and that someone was my wife.

"Violet!" I yelled as I entered Enoch's home, "Where are you?"

"Finn? Oh god, Finn, it's started. The baby is coming." I raced upstairs to find Violet in one of the guest rooms with Enoch holding her hand and a village woman preparing her for birth. Tears streaked her cheeks, and her panic-filled eyes turned on me accusingly.

I replaced Enoch and took her cold, sweaty hand in mine. "I'm here, Vi, and I won't leave, I promise."

"You'd better not—" Whatever she was going to say was

lost with a gut-wrenching scream. Vi's belly rippled with our child trying to find its way out.

"Violet is carrying a large baby. She needs to transition to give birth safely." I turned to see my mother in the doorway. "Seriously? And you couldn't have told me this yesterday?" She ignored my cutting question and moved herself to the other side of Violet and took her other hand.

"Listen to me, my child, breathe wherever I place my hands, breathe deep of the earth." As soon as my mother's hands made contact with Vi's belly, her panic ceased. Violet followed her instructions and calmed down considerably. Everyone left the room, leaving the three of us alone.

"Now listen to me very carefully. You have seen the goddess Gula many times in statues and your dreams. You have painted her, but at the time, you didn't know why the pull was so great. Now that you know she is your mother, you must call on her for the transition to occur and the safe delivery of your child."

"I understand." My wife's violet eyes, and hence her name, gazed on my mother with complete trust.

"Repeat after me... I, Violet, daughter of the goddess Gula and the fallen angel Naberius call upon you, Mother. I, Violet, am ready to become Ninhri, to become my greatest self and transition to become one with my brothers and sisters."

Violet repeated every word that was required. Seconds went by, and I was beginning to wonder if it worked when the air around the bed started to shimmer, then the entire room was filled with tangible sparkles of green and pink, Gula's colors. The goddess appeared and gazed lovingly at her daughter. She placed a hand upon her brow and spoke in a language that sounded Enochian in origin. Then she disappeared.

Violet's body began to tremble and not with our baby, but

with something else. Her violet eyes flew wide, and as she gazed at me, I saw the sparkles that had been in the room in the depths of her irises. With her arms spread wide, Violet was lifted upwards and she hung in space as the energy moved in and around her with increasing speed.

The finality was when her toes and fingers seemed to shoot power into the room and hit me with a bolt, sending me back against the wall behind me while my mother remained utterly unaffected as she replaced her hands on my wife's womb.

"Now, push."

Vi bore down and, with her newfound strength, gave a mighty push, and a moment later, the cries of a new life filled the bedroom. We had done it, created life. I moved beside my mother while she looked after the baby, and then she placed my daughter in my arms.

I held a miracle, our miracle. Her skin glowed, and a white aura surrounded her. Our daughter was a radiant little flower... Zara, the name permeated my consciousness, and when I handed her to Violet, I said, "Meet your daughter, Zara."

"I love it. Hello, little Zara," she cooed. There was a knock on the door.

"It's just me with fresh sheets."

"Come in, Gildas," I called.

"I'll just leave these here," he said, glancing anxiously at the bed.

"Come meet Zara."

Gildas smiled and moved tentatively towards the bed. "Oh my, she is a little beauty, isn't she? I love the name. She looks like a Zara."

"Doesn't she just?" Violet commented dreamily.

"Should I inform everyone? They are all waiting at the bottom of the stairs and anxious for news."

"Violet, are you ready to let your family meet the baby?"

"Maybe take Zara to meet everyone so I can get cleaned up?"

My mother and Gildas stayed to take care of my wife while I descended the stairs to find my brother and his wife, Enoch and his wife, and my father, all with big smiles. "I would like to present Zara Gaea Ackles." My sister-in-law, Lillith, swooped in, taking Zara in her arms. "She is so beautiful, Finn. Congratulations."

Zara opened her eyes, and that's when we all noticed they were gold.

Chapter 14

Jax/Metatron

After my turn holding baby Zara, I escaped outside for some much-needed silence. And not just from the voices that filled Enoch's home, but the super-charged energy those voices belonged to. Life had been pretty quiet this past year, granting all the immortals a reprieve from chaos. Business and life with my wife had been my focus, and now suddenly, everything had changed in a matter of days, and I just needed a few minutes of ordinary.

I walked down to our guest's home and sat down on the porch swing. The sanctuary community was currently quiet, and for once, I was grateful. I knew Lil wanted a baby, and pushing her way in to hold the new one was more evidence of her feelings.

Despite the amount of sex we had, Lillith had not gotten pregnant. We thought she was at our wedding, but she was late, and probably due to the stress of the wedding that had caused her to feel ill at that time. Not the morning sickness she had hoped for.

As a man, I felt many things were spiraling out of my control. I didn't like not being in control. I was the eldest and had no offspring, whereas my younger brother now had a daughter, and my sister had twins. It didn't seem right.

As a brother, a mighty angel, and an immortal, I felt compelled to be on my A-game. Lil and I were on equal footing as a couple, but I always protected her as a husband and did my best to ensure her life was everything she wanted. The luggage was proof of that.

What was bothering me was that our lives felt out of control. Lil and her stuff were ridiculous. She had grown up wealthy and an only child, and it showed that she was spoiled, and she would push for a baby because she wanted one, but did she really?

We had never had the conversation, but I suspected my wife wanted what my siblings had simply because they had it, and she didn't. A part of me wondered if I should have taken a firmer hand with her like Iver had with Isabelle. But then I thought of Finn and Violet, and they didn't have that type of relationship at all. They operated as a couple on a level playing field.

So what was bothering me then? I thought back to our wedding night and the paddles I'd had made exclusively for our first night as husband and wife. They were meant as an experiment at the time, and I found out that Lillith wanted a man who would put her in her place when she really needed it when it came down to the crunch. Was the excess luggage a cry for help, and I'd missed it?

My mind skipped to the past few months. With the constant expansion of Iver's businesses, I had been swamped, and often, Lil had been left to her own devices. As I trusted her completely, this did not bother me, but I was curious about how she had spent her time.

I pulled out my satellite phone and went into our bank

account. Lil had spent large amounts of money at the Sumer Spa. Then I found a bill from a club for three thousand dollars. What? What was she drinking, cocktails made from plutonium? I scrubbed my hands over my face. What was going on?

You know what's going on; wake up.

Metatron, could you be a little clearer?

Your wife is unhappy and is chasing physical pleasure, trying to fill a void. You may want to consider some life changes if you want to keep your marriage happy.

Damn, I pushed Metatron out of my head and stood to go look for my wife, when I spotted her coming down the path.

Lillith joined me on the swing. "You took off pretty fast. Is something wrong?"

"Yes, you could say that."

As Lillith's feet didn't reach the porch, I continued to keep the swing in motion while contemplating my following words.

"What's this about, Jax?"

"Many things, and I think it's time you spent some time being encouraged to be honest. So let's go inside, and after you have had a thorough session with *Daddy's Discipline,* you can confess all your sins, little girl."

Despite the seriousness of my words, Lil's pupils dilated. My wife loved sex and role play, and I was grateful, but I didn't want her turned on so much as submitting to me. I hadn't discovered the joys of role play until I met her. We'd had some crazy sessions together, and it always brought us closer together. Almost as if by playing roles, we learned each other better.

I stood up and took her hand, and we went inside. "I want you naked and in that corner, and you have two minutes." When she was in the proper position in the bedroom corner, I rifled through my suitcase, finding the paddles.

While not overly large, the bedroom had a king-sized bed

and a lovely bench that sat at the end. I pulled that out and placed the paddles on the bed. "Turn around, Lillith, and crawl over here, then place yourself over the bench."

She sauntered like the seductress she was, even sexier on her knees than walking. I realized that this was a game to her, and I wasn't doing myself any favors by approaching the issues this way.

"Stop. Put on a robe, and meet me in the living room." She looked surprised but got to her feet as I fled the bedroom and waited on the couch.

"What's going on, Jax? You're freaking me out a little."

"We need to talk, Lil, and then we can decide what happens next in the bedroom."

"Okay, what do we need to talk about?"

I allowed Metatron some room within as I stared her down.

She dropped her gaze to the floor. "Is this about the baby thing?"

"Lil, look at me," I commanded. Her eyes flew to mine, and again, I allowed Metatron to assist me in giving her a look that spoke volumes. "It's time you confess what is going on with you and what you have been up to."

A flash of guilt was visible before she schooled her features. "I need context, Jax, I don't know what you're talking about."

Hmm, maybe we needed that paddle session after all. "Start with the Sumer Spa, and then the bar bill."

Her eyes narrowed at me. "We're loaded. Why are my bills a concern?"

Now I was getting pissed off, and keeping my cool was becoming increasingly difficult. "How did you manage to spend three thousand dollars at a bar? It is a simple question, and I want an answer."

Her only response was to pout. I sighed in resignation.

"Lillith, I won't give you what you want until you answer my questions." We faced off in silence, but her body language was vibrating. I made up my mind to try a different tactic.

I stood and allowed Metatron to emerge. "Speak," he uttered with such force that Lil nearly fell off the couch with surprise.

"You've been ignoring me. So, I have been going out and having fun."

I became only me once again and sat back down. "What kind of fun?"

"Drinking, partying, dancing. Nothing bad." She was lying. I could always tell by the set of her mouth.

"And?"

"That's it, I swear."

"That's fifty, Lil. Do you want a hundred?"

"That's not fair." She glared at me.

"Neither is lying to me. What have I done to warrant you lying to me?"

She sighed, sitting back, her defense now down. "Nothing, Jax, it's just me. I've been in a weird place lately, and to find more, uh, satisfaction out of life, I have done some things I'm not proud of." Finally, we were getting somewhere.

"Like?"

"Okay, so the reason the bar bill was so high is I used my debit to get fifteen hundred in cash, to try out some drugs."

Jesus, it was worse than I thought.

"You've been busy, and I've not been as busy, and with Vi being pregnant, Isabelle in Scotland, and my mother in Africa, I've been lonely. The thing is being immortal, the drugs didn't work, so it was a total waste, and I haven't tried it since."

That was a relief, at least. "Lillith, I know this may sound preachy, but you know those things are empty pursuits. Why didn't you talk to me? You should have told me how you were feeling. Just because you don't get a hangover doesn't mean that doing these things are okay."

Lil smiled sadly. "I know. I guess I hoped you'd notice and fix me." She gazed up at me, very much resembling a lost child. This was one of those times, when by her own admission, she was asking me to take her in hand.

"You are a strong woman, Lil. You like to control your life. Why do you need intervention?"

She huffed, "Why can't I just need intervention, like Issy? Why can't I just be lost, and you fix it?"

I wanted to laugh at her pout, but she needed more from me. "Because it's not who you are. I will give you what you need after we have talked it out. Now tell me, why do you want a baby so badly?"

"Because I do."

"That's not an answer, Lil. Do you want a baby because you are the only one who doesn't have one? Because you feel left out? Or because you want to grow a family? Because that takes a lot of work, and you have been able to live a selfish life. Based on your current mindset, it's been worse of late."

She leaned back into the couch. "Okay, here it is. I never wanted to work full time. That is why I worked at Sumer for as long as I could because I never really wanted to go into business for my grandfather despite my education. I like my time to be my own, and you're right. I *am* selfish. I want you to myself all the time, and I don't want to share you with Iver's mega-conglomerate. We haven't been on a trip alone since our honeymoon, and I need some husband time."

I could understand that Lillith was still young and needed me more than I realized. "I'll make you a deal, my little brat. When the war is over, assuming we win, I will take vacation time and take you somewhere special, only the two of us. But now, you have a date with a paddle."

"But—"

I laughed at her expression. "This won't be role-playing, Lil. You have to learn that lying and withholding information from me is not acceptable, do you understand?" She nodded her head, and I knew she needed to release from the burdens, not the guilt she had been carrying for too long on her own. I led Lil back into the bedroom, disrobed her, and placed her in the corner.

I waited ten minutes, giving her time to think about her actions and anticipate her punishment. There would be no dilated pupils this time. She understood where things stood. That didn't mean I wasn't going to reward her for taking her strokes. After all, that was the best part. "It is time for you to make amends, Lillith, and unburden yourself. Come here and place yourself over my lap." I wasn't going to spank her this way initially, but now I knew she needed complete surrender, and the knowledge changed my plan.

Lillith was tiny, and with my sudden transformation growth spurt, our size difference was considerable. With Lil over my lap, she was hanging in space, her toes no longer able to touch the floor.

Despite the severity of our situation, I decided on a warm-up and grabbed number three *For better or worse*. "Lillith, from here on out, you will call me Sir or Daddy, do you understand?"

"Yes, Sir."

"Good girl, now reach down and wrap your hands around the legs of the bench." I adjusted her so she could reach more easily. Now she hung over only one leg. It was shocking to see that my thigh was almost as wide as her torso.

I swung my other leg over hers to keep her in place. I rubbed her creamy soft backside for a moment before I cracked the paddle on her ass. I didn't expect her to have much of a response, as Lil had a high threshold, and that was why I'd invested in six paddles instead of one. Like today, I needed something heavier than we would usually use while playing.

A lovely pink spot appeared as if by magic. I cracked the paddle again until a matching one was on her other cheek. Then I set up a pace, bringing the paddle down on the top of her cheek to the top of her thigh and back up again, then I switched to the other cheek. During all of this, Lil was pretty still but emitted grunts with each swat.

I switched now to number six, Daddy's Discipline, and brought it down with a crack in the center of her ass. Lil screeched at the top of her lungs, and I prayed no one heard. Giving her no mercy, I brought the paddle down repeatedly while she squirmed and squealed and begged. I had no plans to stop until she gave in and surrendered.

"Jax! Please." I brought the paddle down hard on her sit spot.

"What did I tell you to call me?" I cracked it down again.

"Sir, Sir, please stop."

I continued peppering her backside, plagued with images of her drinking and doing drugs in the bar, offering plenty of motivation to ensure I got this right. Lillith was crying, and her backside was a deep beet red, and still, I spanked her.

"I'm sorry, Daddy, so sorry."

Now we were getting somewhere. I stopped my relentless paddling and rested the wood on her burning backside. "What are you sorry about, little girl?"

"Everything," she wailed. "I've been naughty and selfish," she blubbered.

I picked up the paddle, flipping it over. I ran the smooth side over her scorching hot backside. "Dig deeper, brat." I brought the paddle down on the backs of her thighs, and she screamed, kicking frantically to escape the sting of the paddle as I continued to bring it down on her sensitive thighs.

It was while I was spanking up the backs of her legs on the

return punishment that I felt the shift in her energy. I stopped the paddling and waited. I wasn't prepared for the hushed words that came out of her mouth.

"Please, Daddy, I just want to be your good girl. I don't want anything else, just for you to love me and be my Daddy." What the? Did I hear right? I released my leg from hers and sat her up on my lap.

"You need to give me more. What does this look like to you, moving forward?"

Lil gazed down at her hands that were tightly gripped on her lap. Her face was almost as red as her backside. Whatever it was she wanted from me, she had to face her personal demons to share.

"Eye contact, little girl, now explain yourself or back down you go."

Lil lifted her eyes and locked them on mine, her struggle and pain evident in her expression. "Just that, what you just said, I need that from you. I need to be stroked, cared for, and, yes, spoiled. I need to be your little girl and sometimes your bratty girl, and your good girl, and I don't mean I want to be treated as a child. But, I really want to just be yours. I don't want to belong to a company, and I no longer wish to be a liaison, Jax. I just want to make dinner for you or provide dinner and be me and be stroked by my Daddy. Do you understand? I want you to lead and make our decisions. I'm tired, and I don't want to, and it's too much for me. I've changed."

Was my strong wife asking me to be my naturally dominant self and leader in our relationship? I didn't think I was the only one crowing with victory. I was pretty sure Metatron was excited too. "Are you sure this is what you want, Lillith?"

"Yes, Sir."

"In that case, you will give your notice immediately, and when this war is over, you will be given an allowance, and we will go over how you spend your time. Is that what you wish?"

"Yes, Sir."

"Lillith, you know I am dominant by nature, and you can ask my sister. I can be really bossy when I am responsible for someone's everything, and you're asking for a twenty-four, seven power exchange. If you try to take your power back at some point, it could cause some serious issues. That is why I am asking you to be sure."

"I understand."

"Good, then you understand when I tell you I am sending you home in a few days." Her eyes rounded in surprise, but she didn't argue with me. That was a first. The fact she was sitting on a blazing backside might have something to do with her penitent attitude.

"I want you safe and away from what's going down. I can't be worried about your safety. We will discuss your expectations, wants, and desires when I return to you in Scotland, clear?"

"Yes, Sir."

"Good girl. Now, I think it's time for something else."

"Yes, Daddy."

Her pupils dilated, and my cock sprung to attention.

Chapter 15

Isabelle/Sandalphon

I found myself questioning the travel process on our trip to the void and wondering why the first time had been so dramatic in comparison. I had no idea who the creature was who met us on the shore, and as he had presented himself as a giant, the entire experience was unsettling. I wanted to know more about what had happened, but I also didn't want to ask, as I found my grandfather intimidating. So, instead, the question rattled about in my head as our small party entered the kingdom.

The throne room might not be the best description as one tended to imagine a medieval or renaissance-style throne room. But this was the void and a place where imaginary beasts and creatures roamed free... anything was possible. This throne room was not constrained by anything earthly or linear. So things appeared and disappeared, I assumed by Azalthath's will or impulse.

As if by magic, the throne dissolved and turned into a war room, complete with a life-sized map and multiple dimensions showing the heavens. It was worlds within universes on a miniature scale. More questions bubbled inside me regarding my grandfather's powers as we gathered around the map.

"As witnessed by Bazazath, a horde is approaching the third heaven. A horde that will disperse into demon regiments and attack Heaven and Earth on the Blood Moon. This army has been building and gathering fallen and other twisted beings for millenniums." He pointed at my heaven, of which I was the guardian, and as he did, the area came alive with activity, and we could see the swarm.

"Why the third heaven, Grandfather, why not an easier target first?" Finn asked as he studied the map. "Earth is such an easy plane to enter and destroy in comparison, isn't it?"

"There are many factors involved in the strategy the dark ones have chosen. I don't know their leader's mind, but he has the plans in motion. Or, I should say they, as there are two."

"Abel and?" Iver asked.

"Abel and Michael, he has been manipulating the board since the beginning." Beside me, I felt my mother freeze. Michael had fallen in love with her and then attempted to steal her from her mate. When that didn't work, he locked them up.

"But that doesn't make sense," Iver said. "He was sent to Earth to take Centouri and Gaea, after they had been sent to Earth to give birth to the souls of archangels, to rebirth three of the mightiest angels ever created. He didn't erase their memories but only blanketed them. Why would he do that if he is the evil mastermind? It makes no sense."

"Michael cannot be trusted." My father's angry voice spoke up. "That angel is no angel, and your brother is a fool to keep his counsel." His comments were aimed at my grandfather, who nodded his head sagely.

"In answer to your observations, Iver Eriskay, Michael is two, divided. Let me explain this way. When in Heaven,

Michael is a creation of God. He is his right-hand angel, so to speak. He cannot control his actions. He can only do what God bids him do."

"That's it!" I yelled out a little too loudly. "You have just answered the question as to why we three were reborn. It all makes sense now."

Azalthath wore a proud smile on his face. "Please tell the others, Isabelle, as they seem ignorant of the answer, and it is an important fact, don't you agree?" I was embarrassed being singled out and would have stepped back if Iver hadn't been standing beside me and chose that moment to squeeze my hand in encouragement.

"If Michael does not have free will in Heaven and can only do as God commands, then he would have to leave the third kingdom to exercise his own plans." The room was silent, but I watched as everyone started to get the gist of what I was saying. "Michael stole Gaea in an attempt to birth the three archangels with her, thereby controlling the strongest force in Heaven. He knew that, like himself, the archangels were beholden to God and do not have free will, but by killing the angel host and imprisoning the souls, he could have them reborn. That's why when he was told by God to bring Gaea and Centouri to Heaven for trial?" I asked because this was an assumption I was making. "Michael chose not to wipe our memories. He orchestrated this, all of this, in an attempt to control the outcome. If God loses, then Michael wins, If God wins, Michael still wins. Grandfather is right, Michael is two beings, and he has divided them to divide and conquer us and Heaven."

The room was silent as all in attendance contemplated my words. I could see the plan now and scolded myself for not having seen it sooner.

"I have a question," Gaea said, "why me? Was I intended for this purpose, or was it simply serendipity?"

All eyes turned my way. "I'm going to guess, but I suspect Azalthath already knows the answer. Grandfather is as old as the ruler in Heaven, an original being and the last of his kind. Michael wished to harness the power of an original, and the easiest way to do that was by having babies with his daughter. Centouri, of course, got in the way of that plan when he came and rescued you from Michael. That pushed the plan ahead of schedule. I don't think Michael wanted us born yet, and that is when Iver comes in. Michael appeared to Iver and Enoch. In fact, he has always appeared to Enoch, and while not a friend, he has certainly offered him advice and answers. He appeared as a friend to Enoch on purpose. I believe Iver, Enoch's son, was always part of Michael's plan. Anyway, Centouri showing up was completely unexpected, and because Michael lost Gaea, he had no choice but to allow the souls to be born. I assume he hoped to gain our side eventually and have us fight for him."

There was another long pause while the group processed this information. "You know, Michael did us a favor."

"How so?" my father demanded.

"We died so we could have free will, something he will never have." Iver squeezed my hand. If not for the bigger picture, I wouldn't be here, and we wouldn't be married or have children.

"I have free will," Centouri said, "so why do I and none of the other angels?"

"Because, Father, God has presumably set you aside; you are no longer his. I suspect he fully expects you to become a demon. And why he didn't take your wings like everyone else, I have no idea, unless God is privy to Michael's plans and left them intact for a purpose or, and I shudder to think, he has no clue where you are. Maybe he thinks you are still in prison, so your wings are irrelevant."

Everyone started to talk then, debating back and forth

about God and what he might or might not know. I gazed up at Iver, who remained quietly stoic at my side. After some time had passed, our group calmed down, and Grandfather called on everyone's attention.

"I've heard from Yemaya. She and Raphe have found all the living fallen and their firstborns and will join you in Africa within a week."

"How many should we be expecting?" Iver directed his question to my grandfather.

"Many, but we will still be at a huge disadvantage. Now, here is what I see," Azalthath continued, moving the meeting along. "We need to drive the horde, as demons number us five to one at the very least." A collective sigh went up around the table. "And that is based on what we know. We must be prepared for that to double, or even triple."

"That is genocide. How can we fight such a large army?" Jax questioned.

My grandfather turned his eyes on me. "Because you have the Savior on your side. As you know from your battle with Leviathan, Isabelle can control actions with her voice."

"Yes, but that is only humans and immortals. It didn't work on Leviathan, who was a demon," Jax argued.

Azalthath grimaced. It took me a moment to realize this was his version of a human smile. "That was before she bonded with Sandalphon. Even the titans, should they appear, could not gainsay her now."

All eyes turned uncomfortably in my direction. On one side, Iver squeezed my hand in encouragement, and on the other, my mother, surprisingly, did the same.

"Isabelle," she said softly, "for several thousand years, the one god has done everything in his power to subjugate the human race, enslave them to one belief system. There is no one system. It is a lie. The paths to enlightenment are many, and to belong to the light, all one has to do is see the truth. In time, humans will have the scales lifted from their eyes. War and fighting will become a thing of the past. We can restore this planet before it is destroyed and recreated in another galaxy. You, we, are necessary, and the coming days and even the loss is necessary, for if we won't fight for the rights of all living creatures, who will?"

Silence followed her impassioned speech. I knew she was right. We didn't have a choice, and in that way, like Michael, we had no free will. Forces more immense than all of us were herding us to this conclusion, and we had to allow the plan to play out.

Azalthath cleared his throat in a very human parody of gaining our attention. "As I said, Isabelle is the key. She will need to be protected while she does what she can to turn the tides in our favor, and it cannot be the Weigand Baidya." He directed his look to Iver. "I know you were charged with the protection of my granddaughter, but this is your destiny to lead the greatest army in creation."

"I will protect my daughter," Centouri announced. "To my last breath, I will fight to keep her safe."

Azalthath offered my father one of his grimacing smiles. "I thank you, Centouri, but I have another in mind, one whose powers will keep her invisible to the enemy but visible to our army. That is the safest position for her."

"You, Father?" Gaea queried.

"Yes, and I have added an additional cloaking spell on your sanctuary in Africa, Enoch is a powerful angel, but he cannot hide anything from the archangels or Cain and Abel. Yemaya has been told how to bring the immortals into the hidden village, so our numbers remain a secret. Even now, firstborns are transitioning. Iver, you have war leaders and you will need to divide our host. Your old friends are enhanced now, with the inherited powers of their birthright."

It was my turn to squeeze Iver's hand. I knew he was

barely listening, as he was still stuck on not protecting me. My grandfather droned on, either not noticing or not caring about Iver's lack of enthusiasm.

"Albion will be your first general. She has inherited her father's love of thunderbolts and a voice almost as powerful as Isabelle's. Aquarius, no longer Archer, is now a god in his own right and will lead, with the help of Diana, the sneak attack that will help drive the horde to our battlefield on the plains."

"Wait," I called, "Diana? But she doesn't fight. In fact, she can barely protect herself. How could she possibly help Archer?"

"Because, Granddaughter, she is part Diana, the goddess of the hunt. Her mother imbued her with tactical skills that rival Weigand Baidya." That was shocking, and I found it difficult to picture my immortal friends with their new powers, and I wasn't the only one.

"Lucius has been infused with Vidas' powers to control the realms of the air, so he will be best used in the second or third heaven to help fight and manipulate our enemies' movements. That brings me to my grandson." His gaze traveled to Jax. "You will lead the Earth forces, as this is your realm, Metatron, where you're strongest—"

"What about the gods and goddesses? Are they fighting by our side?" Iver interrupted.

Azalthath seemed to ponder his response as we waited, holding our breaths. "Yes, but not all have chosen to help Earth, and they will not fight in troop formation. I'm sure you understand this, Iver, when you are in your other form. Being able to see multiple moves in multiple locations at once allows for a broader vision. As such, the gods can choose where they are most needed. However, they need to heed the leader's voice and come to his aid, which will be agreed upon once everyone arrives. We are done, for now. When the rest arrive, we will have a war council and plans discussed in greater detail."

Everyone stood to take their leave, but I had one more question. "Grandfather, what of your kingdom? You have every manner of beast living here. Will they help?"

"They gave up on the world when man took his position as the lead predator. I can not commit them to fight for a world they gave up on long ago. Here, they will always be protected, in a world with no end or a beginning. In addition to that, they will be protecting a package that is of the utmost importance. I will say no more at this time."

Our group traveled in silence to the gates of my grandfather's realm. Lost in their own thoughts, no doubt of what was shared at the council table. But I knew in my heart the truth. I had the power to make them fight if I had to, and I would before I lost Earth and made anyone left alive slaves to the dark.

Chapter 16

Iver/ Weigand Baidya

Our warriors arrived at the sanctuary in small groups, under cover of a powerful cloaking spell provided by the ancient god Azalthath. Raphe and his mother, Yemaya, were first, after completing their mission to find all the hidden immortals and their firstborns.

Yemaya and my mother-in-law disappeared into the jungle soon after Yemaya's arrival to do what, who knew? It had been too long since I'd seen Raphe. He, Jax, and I sat around a campfire, drinking whiskey and discussing his trip. "Why isn't Diana with you?'

"She is with her mother. They will arrive together in a day or two."

"Tell us," Jax sat forward, "has she changed much? You know, now that she is infused with her goddess traits."

Raphe laughed. "Diana has changed, but not in ways I'm going to share with you." We were into our third bottle of whiskey when Manakel, Orion, and Asher, with their transformed firstborns, and with them their mated goddesses, Cymopoleia, Asteria, and Eos, arrived.

With the arrival of the restored fallen, an unreal quality began to imbue the compound and village. Seeing fallen with wings, when for millenniums, there had been none, was breathtaking, and this included my father. With each new arrival, Isabelle, Jax, and Finn seemed to retreat into themselves.

I knew they were struggling, and unlike everyone else, they'd only known their dual selves for a short window of time. They were raised as humans and recently merged with their archangel soul. Finn had transitioned long before Jax and my wife, but Isabelle and Jax had equal responsibilities to me on the fighting field, and unlike me, they had never been in battle. I wanted to protect them and not let them fight and had they simply been immortals, I could have. But each of them had a role to play in the upcoming war.

As fallen, firstborn, and deities arrived in numbers, what the siblings had only read about in fairy tales and myths was very real and walking among them. It was a lot to take in.

I kept it real with my wife, as did our children, keeping her grounded. Unlike Isabelle, the twins seemed more like the gods and goddesses than she or I. I'd lived my life for thousands of years as an immortal with some skills, but our children knew in the womb who they were, and their acceptance of the players surrounding us was putting added pressure on my wife.

Finn was making plans to send Violet home with his new daughter and Lillith and Sheila, Lil's mom. Gaea and Centouri spent a lot of their time with the twins, leaving Isabelle biting her nails and questioning herself and everything she once believed in.

At the end of the long line of guests, my mother, Freya, arrived without her wolf, Vanargand. Instead, she had my family with her, a half-dozen demigods from Norse mythology. The Vanir deities were not a warrior race. They were gods of guardianship and creation. The warrior gods, like Thor, were from the first family, the Aesir.

Having Freya in the flesh for longer than a few stolen moments was a fervent prayer answered, a dream come true. "Where is Vanargand?"

"Do you really need to ask?" She pointed at my chest?

"I ignorantly didn't realize that by bonding with Vanargand, he would be removed from your pet from your side. For that, I apologize."

"Don't, the wolf was always meant to be in you, my son. Now, where is your wife? I would like to meet the Savior in person." As if by saying the word *Savior*, Isabelle heard and walked towards us, and with her, the twins.

My mother smiled at the trio, welcoming Isabelle with a hug. Then she effortlessly lifted both my children into her arms.

"Arkyn, Deva, I am your grandmother, Freya." As if rehearsed, the twins leaned their foreheads against my mother's. A blue light enveloped the three for a split second and then dissipated. She placed them back on the ground.

"What was that? What did you do to my children, Freya?" Isabelle's wide, frightened eyes moved from me to my mother for an explanation.

She ignored Isabelle and spoke to the children in old Norse. When they responded in kind and then left giggling, I knew what she had done.

"You imprinted on them and gave them their Nordic history?"

"I did," she answered, speaking directly to Isabelle. "They now know our history from the beginning, the secrets of the gods, and our languages. But most importantly, when they need their family, if something ever happened, we could intervene."

Isabelle liked this answer and nodded her head. "That is good, for our children are at a great risk, aren't they?"

"Only in this realm, Savior. The twins can access multiple dimensions. Nothing is stopping them from traveling through the universe."

Isabelle stood still, appearing thoughtful. "I see, well, then I thank you, as it seems inevitable that one day, maybe sooner than expected, their parents won't be capable of saving them." She turned and walked after the twins.

I wanted to follow her, but my mother grabbed my arm. "Let her go, son. She has to figure out her strength for herself. And she will when it counts, I assure you."

I escorted my mother and her fellow gods to their temporary housing, with promises of a large courtyard dinner later that day. Then I went off in search of the source of the yelling I heard on my way back to the training compound.

I arrived in time to see my wife, in her form-hugging shorts and tank top, drenched in sweat, covered in dirt, and fighting with Archer. Now in his fully evolved god version, he was like Permelus on steroids. Archer, Permeleus, had always been the deadliest warrior on Earth, but he'd never been a large man. He was now. Aquarius looked like a golden hero, how Hercules used to look in his early days of glory. There wasn't a woman present, goddess or not, who hadn't soaked their panties watching him move.

Archer had always been gorgeous and a fighting machine, but as a god, he was so much more, ethereal and the true embodiment of an ancient warrior king. By comparison, with her human constraints no longer holding her back, Isabelle moved, a silver streak of light as she fought, while Aquarius pushed her, demanding performance, as he yelled out commands. I had never wanted her as badly as I did right then. The fact that the watchers were all salivating didn't help.

In another sparring match, Lucius fought Diana. The goddess Diana called out commands as her daughter flexed her muscles against Luci. His outward appearance hadn't changed much, but Luci was already large and deadly. His eyes seemed different, and I wondered if melding with his goddess mother's powers had softened his character somewhat. Out of our core group, Luci had always had the most challenging time. He never really belonged anywhere, always wandering, looking for a battle, but now, he seemed to have more precision. His movements almost articulated a greater intelligence. I was lost, watching him move, so similar but so very different than I'd ever seen.

Tabbris, Luci's fallen father, appeared at my side. "He is fighting different," I commented, "more precise."

Tabbris chuckled. "His mother's influence."

"Is she here?"

"Oh, yes, off fornicating with someone, no doubt. I don't know if you've noticed, but the immortals are pairing off. If our world lives after the war, there will be many newborns." I was about to respond when Tabbris patted me on the back and moved towards the trees on the other side of the compound. Standing in wait, was my mother.

"Iver, your mother is mating with Tabbris. Isn't that going to be a problem?" Isabelle was with me and whispering so as not to be overheard.

I gazed down at my sweaty, dirty girl and laughed. "Isabelle, they can hear you so you can stop whispering."

She blushed.

"Tabbris is a powerful fallen. Why wouldn't she? This is how it is done, Isabelle. As the daughter of the Earth goddess, haven't you felt a pull to copulate?"

Her color deepened to a deep puce. "I, uh, yes, of course, but no more than usual."

I raised my eyebrow at her blatant lie.

"I could have sex all day long, to be honest, but I only feel attracted to you. Why is that? Not that I'm complaining."

My turn to gloat. "I guess I'm just that good."

She smacked my arm playfully.

"We're different than the rest of those here, Isabelle. We have marked each other, and we floated when it happened, remember? That is a life union. You are stuck with me." I meant it to be funny, but she seemed worried instead of amused.

"Iver, do you want to have sex with the goddesses? I mean, is there someone here you want to mate with?"

"No, my mate is all I need, and I need her now." I scooped her up and, as I took off, evolved into Weigand Baidya. I felt free as the air moved through my wings, carrying us deep into the uncharted Congo. I knew of a cave where I had hidden with Raphe and my father a few thousand years earlier when we were running from a particularly nasty demon who had it in for Raphe.

The cave had its own ecosystem and was covered in soft moss. I placed Isabelle down on the soft green carpet and stood back from her. I didn't attempt to shapeshift back to my human form. Isabelle eyed me questioningly. "I want to take you in my wolf form, but I want your permission and your submission."

Isabelle stripped off her sweaty garments and dropped to her knees, bowing her head. "Yes, please, I've wanted you as Weigand Baidya since the first time you changed. Take me."

I dropped my giant muzzle and wrapped my powerful jaws around her neck. I didn't squeeze as she'd already given her submission. Her body stilled as she waited for me to make my next move.

I placed my large paw on her back and was surprised to see it covered the width and almost the entire length of her back. I pressed her chest to the ground. "Stay," I commanded, then backed a few feet away, nuzzling her entrance with my wet nose. Isabelle gasped at the cold pressing against her hot entry but stayed in position.

I licked her with my tongue, tasting her essence. My wolf senses were more enhanced, and the subtleties of her hidden notes were no longer so subtle. My mate had delicious under-notes of vanilla bean, fruit, and some exotic heady flower I couldn't name.

My body convulsed with need, and I dug my tongue into her hot channel. Isabelle moaned loudly as she opened wider, lifting her needy core higher. I nipped at her bud and caught her essence as it gushed on my tongue. My animal was panting with the need for release. I kept him at bay while I continued to stroke her with my tongue, meting out so much pleasure that she orgasmed with each lick.

But the crux of giving cunnilingus in my wolf form was my roughened tongue. Soon the pleasure I was meting out would change to torment. My tongue would feel like sandpaper, and her swollen lips and nub would be on fire.

I was ready to take her everywhere and own her as a wolf. I crouched over her raised ass and began to sink my cock into her. Isabelle let out a keening that seemed to come from the very depths of her being.

"Iver, you're so big, oh my god!" she screamed as I squeezed her neck with my powerful jaws and sunk all the way inside her. I let out a howl and began slowly fucking her. "Iver, I feel drunk. I can barely stay on my knees. I, oh!" she shouted again as she came all over me.

I wasn't ready to let up. I wanted to claim Isabelle's ass, and the next time she spilled, I pulled out and used my tongue to run her lovely juices up her seam to her puckered anal opening. After laving her entrance a few times, I pressed inside her, slowly, filling her so completely that she couldn't move, couldn't push back, rendered immobile. My wolf wanted me to take her hard, but my humanness calmed the raging beast.

"Do you feel that, little immortal, that is my cock taking you, owning you, every damn inch of your body is mine to do with as I please."

"Yes," she panted. "Yes, yes, yes, anything, just don't stop!" she cried out as she orgasmed. While I was lodged fully inside, I changed back to mortal and began to pump her hard. I slapped her ass repeatedly while I thoroughly took her. "Iver, I-I-I don't know how much more I can take."

"You have submitted to my will. I know when you have had enough." I reddened her backside with several stinging blows. "Understand?" I asked as she screamed with her release and collapsed on the moss beneath her. She was a mess of grunts, squeals, and mewls that crescendoed with an explosive orgasm that overtook her. That's when I let go with a shout, filling her tight ass with my seed. We lay trembling in the aftermath for quite some time before either of us spoke.

"Iver?"

"Yes, my little goddess?"

"I like you, but I really like your wolf too."

I laughed and nipped her shoulder. "My wolf likes you too, Isabelle. Now, can you move, or do you want to stay here?" I was answered by her gentle snores. "Here, it is then." I wrapped my arm around her and tucked her body into me as tightly as I could to keep her warm. And just before slumber took me, I felt like the universe was lining up for the first time.

Chapter 17

Gaea

Our band of immortals, gods, and goddesses had traveled to see my father in his kingdom for a war council. Although the gods knew of his kingdom, no one had been invited to see it until now. I don't know who was more shocked with each other's appearance, the varied creatures he harbored, or the gods who thought they had died out long ago.

The mingling was like no other in the history of creation, and as an entity that loved the natural world beyond all else, it warmed my heart and gave me hope for the future.

I insisted that we bring the twins. It was time for Arkyn to meet his destiny. Freya had tried explaining to Iver what would come to pass, but his brain hadn't accepted her words, or maybe he hadn't been ready. Time was running out for Iver and Isabelle to acknowledge and support Arkyn's destiny as the greatest ruler and my father's successor. Arkyn would be king of the Earth and the veil, uniting all kingdoms, and finally, all creatures would have peace.

Arkyn's child brain had no problem understanding and accepting this knowledge and knew in his heart what he was, although he didn't have the language to share it with his parents yet. Iver and Isabelle believed that Centouri and I spent so much time with the children to bond and connect, which, in essence, was the truth, but in addition, we were teaching and testing them for their future roles.

Isabelle and Iver would do what they had been doing naturally since they came together, be the king and queen of the immortals, run the economy of the earth, and drive the corporate and political world.

Jax, my eldest, would continue as Iver's right-hand man. It was up to me to ensure Lillith would be an asset to this inevitability, and as such, I arranged a private luncheon, while Centouri would spend time with Jax, following our meeting in the veil.

"Hello?" She was right on time.

"In the back," I called. I wanted to own the space in which we would dine, which meant I controlled the setting, energy, and conversation and directed it where I needed it to go. I had to complement Enoch for his vision of this compound. He'd done such a lovely job of maintaining the natural integrity of the land and its local offerings that I felt like I was living in a wild game preserve.

I observed Lillith as she made her way down the path to where I waited for her. When we first met, Lillith emanated power, and I'd felt she would feel more at home in a power suit than her khaki ensemble. But now, she seemed different, no less potent in her skimpy summer frock that couldn't hide her curves and feline energy, more content, less anxious. Something had changed since last I saw her.

"Good afternoon, Mother. I was happy to receive an invite to lunch. Is it just us?" she asked, gazing at the setting for two.

"It is, just us girls. I wanted to get to know you better."

Her eyes landed on the white wine that Gildas was pour-ing. He had offered to serve us luncheon, and I had agreed. The man was a gift with a heart for service, and I enjoyed his energy. "Is that Domaine Leflaive Batard Montrachet?" Lillith asked excitedly.

I nodded. "Wow, this is a coveted bottle of wine, and very expensive." Lillith took her seat and the proferred wine glass. "Thank you, Gildas, and you, Mother. Shall we toast?"

"Yes, to life's simple pleasures."

Lil mimicked the toast, and we clinked our stemware, the resounding ching resonating through the clearing. She dropped her head back and savored the flavors.

"Can you taste the subtle hints of lemon and hazelnut?"

"Oh, yes, it's like an erotic dance on one's tongue," Lillith responded, her eyes hooded in pleasure. She was a sexual being, that was for sure.

We chatted about minor things, engaging in polite conver-sation until our meal was finished. Then we relaxed with coffee from Isabelle's plantation. "This coffee really is deli-cious. I heard you helped in creating a business plan for acquiring the coffee plantation. Is that your first independent company acquisition?"

Lillith blushed. "I helped Isabelle with the financials in acquiring and running the plantation, and we worked out a five and ten-year expansion plan to help the local economy. The rest was Iver, who is the expert in all things business."

I let loose a tinkling laugh that drew responses from the forest. Lillith's eyes rounded with polite inquisitiveness at the sudden chattering from the forest. "I hear Iver isn't the only business expert. My son is his right-hand man, is he not?"

"Yes, Jax has amazing instincts. I imagine that will have increased now that he has transformed? Is that right? Will his instincts sharpen?" She wanted to know, that much was obvi-ous, but I couldn't give her the answer she desired.

"Yes, everything enhances. I'm sure you noticed," I winked at her, and she blushed, reaching for her coffee to hide her embarrassment.

"Um, yes, he is very much enhanced. I guess I'm wondering what's next for us. He is a man and an archangel. How does that work for me? I'm just an immortal with nothing special to offer."

Now I had her right where I needed her to be. "Lilith, you have a critical job that only you can do. Jax is your destiny, love, and you two will produce a brood of children who will one day take over the running of Iver's kingdom, which will encompass the entire world by then. You were made for Metatron, only you, and no one else."

Happy tears trickled down Lillith's beautiful porcelain skin. "I'm so happy, thank you. I love him so much, and I was afraid I would no longer fit his needs."

I laughed. "Oh, from what he says, you are more than capable of fitting his needs. Now, no more worrying. Life is a brilliant, beautiful gift, Lillith, and it's time you started to see that. When are you flying to Scotland?"

"Tonight." Lillith was anxious, probably worried about what would happen to her man.

"Darling girl, your man will be safe, I promise. Remember, you can't have a host of babies without him. Even now, your body is humming with new life and can expect twin girls in about seven and a half months."

"What? Eek," she screamed, "yes, yes, yes!" Lillith fist-pumped the air and jumped up, doing a little dance. A thought brought her up short, and she sat back down. "What about Isabelle and Iver? Will they survive?"

I knew there were two possible outcomes for my daughter and her extraordinary man. I knew this because I saw no more children in their future. "I have not seen their future, Lil, only yours. When you're home in Scotland, I want you to surround yourself with only good things, walk, swim, eat, sleep, read, meditate, do yoga, and connect with your roots. Too long, you have lived in the concrete jungle, and it is time for self-nurturing. I promise I will be there for the birth of your twin girls."

A huge grin lit up Lillith's face. "Thank you, Mother, your words have meant so much to me, more than I could ever express. I needed to hear your message, and I'm so grateful you invited me to lunch."

We parted ways a short time later, and I moved out to the shade to meditate and talk to nature. I needed conditions for the day of the battle, and the earth would help me make that happen.

Chapter 18

Finn/Bazazath

After consulting with my grandfather, it was decided that Violet and our new baby daughter, Zara, should fly home to Scotland and stay protected by Serge and a host of other immortals who would not be fighting in the war. Sheila and Lillith would be going to Scotland with them.

After seeing the family off safely, I knew it would be time for Iver to bring Arkyn and Deva to the void, as it was the only place the demon horde couldn't get to them. We stood watching Isabelle spar with Freya. She and the other gods had been helping to hone her skills and those of the transformed fallen.

"We're ready, Finn," Violet called. I ascended the stairs and took Zara from my wife's arms, hopefully, not for the last time. I kissed her little forehead, and her golden eyes opened and regarded me. Her little face was mine looking back at me. I was told by Gaea that happened with newborns. They were meant to reflect their fathers. An age-old gene cycle that had existed since the beginning of time when DNA testing didn't exist.

I grabbed the suitcase in my other hand, and we made our way downstairs and out to the Jeep, where the family was waiting to say goodbye.

"Auntie Violet," the twins said in unison.

Violet smiled down at the children. "Yes, my dear hearts, what is it?"

Each one took hold of a leg and hugged. "Don't worry, we'll take care of Uncle Finn."

I put the suitcase down, and when Vi took the baby, I reached down, scooped up the giggling twins, and threw one over each shoulder. "You will, will you? Then tell me, who is going to take care of you two rascals?"

I shouldn't have asked because they chimed, "Grandfather," in unison.

"Iver, what are they talking about?" Isabelle asked.

"Let's go and have a chat, Isabelle. Finn, you good here?" he asked, turning a pleading look my way.

I wanted to laugh. The only thing that could scare the great Weigand Baidya was his angel wife.

Clearly, he still hadn't told her, and the battle was the next day at dawn. I decided to play along and act ignorant, so my sister didn't kill me. "You two go chat. I've got these monsters."

Iver left, holding Isabelle's hand, to draw her away from the group to talk. It was probably for the best, as their 'talks' usually ending up in loud sex.

"While this is a lovely goodbye," Jax commented, watching his sister walk away, "we need to get a move on. The jet is fueled and waiting for you."

I leaned down to kiss Violet and Zara, and the twins did too as they were still in my arms. Jax kissed Lil and told her not to worry. As they loaded themselves in the Jeep, Lil called out, "Wait, I have news, an added reason to make sure this Neanderthal makes it home alive…" Lillith gazed at Jax lovingly.

"Yes," Jax added. "Lillith is pregnant, six weeks along, and with twins. Looks like you two," he looked at Arkyn and Deva, "will have little twin cousins to boss around in about eight months."

The twins clapped their hands in excitement. With a final wave, the two Jeeps loaded with passengers and luggage pulled out of the compound.

My heart was heavy with the separation from Violet and Zara, the physical loss of their company weighing on me. But they would be safe, and that was what was most important. They would be waiting for me when the war was over, and hopefully, we would be the victors.

"Jax, come on, brother, let's go over tactical one more time. After all, you have a legion to lead." Jax finally swung his eyes away from the gate and to me, and I saw in his eyes the same conflict I was feeling and something else, determination.

"Good idea, let's go. Iver, are you coming?"

Iver shook his head. "I have a couple of items that need my attention before I move into full battle gear. I'll meet up with you later." He took the twins from my arms and I wondered what type of goodbye they would have? At least Lil and Violet were safe and away from harm. But Isabelle was also a mother, and much of the final outcome was dependant on her.

We left the family of four and made our way down to the training grounds. The gods and goddesses weren't present, but all the fallen and firstborns were in attendance. "Where's Iver? Raphe asked when he spotted us.

"He and Issy are taking the twins to safety and will be along shortly."

Jax fixed his eyes on me. "Where are they going, Finn?"

"To our grandfather, more specifically, to the void, the only place the demon horde can't get them."

"Seriously? Why didn't you tell me before? I should have said goodbye when I had the chance."

"Isabelle didn't know. Well, I guess she is finding out now, and she won't be happy about it. But think, brother, if we lose, the twins will be destroyed. Remember what Centouri told us, Arkyn will one day be king. Do you know what that means?" Jax looked thoughtful and then shrugged.

"I thought he meant he would one day take over Iver's role, but after Lil had lunch with our mother today, she told her that our children would take over the empire. So, no, I have no idea what Centouri was talking about."

I sighed. Jax was such a linear thinker. "Arkyn will rule Earth and the places in between, he will be the ultimate king, and Deva will someday replace Gaea."

Jax's eyes grew wide.

"Are you serious? If that's true, then Arkyn will become—"

"God," I interrupted, "and, yes, he will ascend, and we will one day be his servants, but only if we win. The horde is at our doors because the power of the alien in the sky is waning. He is disappearing, which is what all this is about. The universe needs a new leader, a new creator, one whose care for all beings is not centered only on humans made in an image, but who sees all creatures fairly and equally."

"Wow, so Isabelle, she's going to lose her shit."

I laughed at his words. "Yeah, that is exactly what Iver said. But he also added that in the end, Isabelle would fall in line with the plan, and if anyone can get her to submit to the will of the universe's plan, it is Iver."

Jax laughed. "Isabelle is the most stubborn person I have ever met."

I nodded in agreement. "She is, but it is this unwillingness to lose that makes her so powerful. I don't think we could win this war without her."

"I agree. Now, let's go check in with our warriors."

Chapter 19

Isabelle/Sandalphon

When Iver squeezed my hand, I knew I wouldn't like whatever plan he had concocted with my grandfather and Iver knew it. I waited until we were a distance away from the two Jeeps and our departing family.

I glared at him. "What have you done?" I demanded.

"Nothing, yet. But I think when I share with you what your grandfather has shared with me, you will agree that it all makes sense."

I tapped my foot impatiently. The truth was I already knew, but I was playing stupid. Even I knew that the twins would be killed by the demons if they got their hands on them. They were the most vulnerable, especially if either one of us was taken captive or killed. That didn't mean I liked it, and I didn't, not one bit. "Just say it, Iver, rip off the damn band aid."

"We don't have much time, Isabelle, I can feel the darkness descending on Earth like a large, evil blanket. We need to take the twins to the void, your grandfather can hide them, and the creatures of the void will protect them with their lives, I swear it."

"Fine."

Iver's expression was so comical, I would have laughed outright if the topic hadn't been so dire. My brothers walked by then, dropping the twins into Iver's arms, and kept on walking.

"See you two when you get back, "Jax called back. Finn punched him in the arm and sent Iver an apology smile over his shoulder.

Brothers. I shook my head. I swear, the older they got, the more annoying they became.

"Fine? What do you mean fine? Like no argument kinda fine?"

I couldn't help myself, I finally let out the laughter I'd been holding in, and the twins joined me. I assumed they had no idea what I was laughing about, and my humor was simply a trigger for theirs.

Iver watched, his expression moving through several transitions before landing on a blend of amused annoyance. "You knew."

"Sure did. I mean, really, was there any other choice?"

"Oh, sure, I've been torturing myself for days over how to explain this to you," he huffed.

"I know." I grinned. "And it was so much fun to watch, to be honest. But the fun and games are over, so we'd better get a move one." I set the twins down. "Go say goodbye to your grandparents, children."

They scampered off, and Iver leaned in close to me. "Isabelle."

"Yes, my love?"

"When this is all over, and you're tied to my bed, I'll get you back for this."

I felt my seam moisten at the threat growled from his sexy, commanding voice.

"I certainly hope so… Sir."

Iver gave me a positively primal smile, then taking my hand, we went off to get the twins and take them to my grandfather. When we came back, we had the battle to prepare for.

Chapter 20

Gaea

I t seemed that only moments after my daughter and Iver returned from the void, the world descended into darkness. The news and social media were reporting an unusual eclipse prior to the Blood Moon. But for us in the supernatural world, we knew this was the work of Abel, blackening out the sky to intimidate us before battle.

Abel wasn't the only one with a trick or two up his sleeve. Yemaya had joined me in gathering vital energy from the earth's resources. With that complete, and my grandchildren all safely tucked away, my concern was my daughter, Isabelle. She would need to be where the action was the hardest, which meant she would be moving between the battle in the third plain and the one on Earth. I knew she could do it, and I knew she could win, but only if she dug deep. Holding her back was a concern for her family, most especially for Iver and her brothers. Ironically, she needed to harness that fear and concern and use it.

I understood as I had watched many family members decimated by wars. My father and I were all that remained of the originals. Everyone else had perished a long time ago. My children and grandchildren were more precious than they realized, and I planned on enjoying them for as long as possible.

We moved out to the plains, while around us, the jungle was eerily silent. I had told all of its beautiful creations to hide in the deepest part of the Congo and be still. They were not to come out unless I summoned them, but I prayed it wouldn't come to that.

My husband stood beside Finn, ready to fight, his great wings folded back. His face looked blank, at least to the casual observer, but I knew him well. Centouri was moving inwards to a place of mechanics. He fought in the last great war, as had all of the fallen. But I knew he was worried about facing off with Michael.

We had to assume that Michael would be fighting for the opposing team. Isabelle caught my eye and placed her hand on her heart then, like a rocket, took off, disappearing from sight with a host of fallen that included Aquarius and Diana. Aleena was not here to see her man off, as she had nothing to transition into. She had been born Eve, and while the oldest immortal on Earth, she was not privy to a metamorphosis like the rest. Raphe, however, was staring into the sky long after Diana disappeared.

He wasn't the only one; Weigand Baidya watched his wife's departure, his expression giving away nothing, but his mournful howl filled the night with his frustration at not being with her. Jax saluted and took his forces to the air, waving his mighty hammer as he flew. To human eyes, the battle in the sky would be invisible, but the deities would be able to follow them on multiple fronts at once.

Finally, Weigand Baidya moved the largest of the force into position, with my father beside him. He would keep us all invisible until the last minute. Yemaya turned her almond eyes to me. "It is time, Gaea. We must be ready."

I nodded and we moved to the far side of the plains, far behind the war party. I changed my form, as did Yemaya, and we would be nothing more than specs of dust. As we arrived, great orange flames shot from the heavens. Freya, with her band of warriors, flanked Weigand. While just above them, Enoch hovered with some of his fallen, throwing energy balls made of Elysium at the demons. Those in the direct path of the balls burned in a white fire before exploding into silver dust. I was told that was important; otherwise, the demons could rejuvenate themselves, and we didn't need to fight them more than once.

Never had I seen so many demons. For every immortal, there seemed to be fifty of the nasty things. Lucius had taken the rear and was under heavy attack by those demons who had circled around.

I summoned the earth to me, filling the demons with dirt and sand, blinding them, and allowing our force to fight free of the enclosed circle they had been trapped in only moments ago. Yemaya moved around some distance away, duplicating, and each time we found a swarm, we gathered the dust of the earth to blind our enemies.

Back during the first war, there had not been Elysium, although the angels carried weapons imbued with something similar, and I found it odd now that where the demons fell, there was nothing left but silver particles that mingled with the sands on the plain. I imagined in a war of humans, the sand would have rivers of blood running through it.

I glanced up when the shards of light filtering through the dark were suddenly gone, shrouding us again in complete darkness. Abel had arrived and was facing off against my son. Abel had Isabelle's gift and rendered Jax's hold while he swept his mighty sword through the air, the intention clear, to swipe off Jax's head. From somewhere, I heard Isabelle bark out a command in the language of the angels. And at the last second, Jax's mighty hammer rose and clashed against Abel's sword.

The air above our heads cracked with the mighty blows, while Isabelle's voice filled the atmosphere. I couldn't understand all she said, but as she poured out her song, the heavens parted, and down appeared Michael, his flaming sword drawn and aimed at my daughter's head. A howl went up from Iver, a warning.

Isabelle continued to sing, not missing a beat as she fought Michael in single combat. Tears poured from my eyes in both horror and respect for what was unfolding. My daughter was unlike any power, and watching her fight for the world, her family, and friends was beyond beautiful. It was the essence, the very fabric of life swirling like a whirling dervish, and I knew I was witnessing a single-handed clash of magnanimous proportions that hadn't been seen since our originals set foot here on Earth.

No one would know of this fight. She wouldn't be in the history books, like Permelus had a lifetime ago, when he trained the great Achilles. No, Isabelle would never be known in that way, but the supernatural plain would never forget, and she would become the stuff of legends.

Even from this distance, I could see that Isabelle was tiring. She couldn't keep up her song and fight Michael. I wasn't the only one who saw her tiring. Michael grinned, shifting into a massive demon, and finally, we knew the end game. This had all been about ending resistance to him taking over everything. By getting us all out in the open at once, he could end anyone who stood in his way. Michael hadn't been an angel. He'd been the devil himself and would enslave Earth and all its creatures, and as the new God, he would subjugate the human race.

On the plains, the demons howled with glee as Isabelle was slashed by the flaming sword. Iver was about to take off into the air, but his mother and her tribe held him back. This was not his fight, it belonged to the gatekeepers, and from out of nowhere, Finn showed up, the demon killer. Now that Michael had shown us his proper form, Finn could end his life.

The siblings now moved in an intricate war dance as they fought against the beast. Isabelle's voice grew louder until her voice no longer sounded as if it came from her. Looking for the source of the amplification, I saw my father adding his power to hers. Now, she directed the fight in all realms. Her voice rang out, filling space and time in both the celestial plains and the one of Earth. She and Finn fought, and every time one of them was stabbed by Michael's flaming sword, the horde on Earth cheered. I knew without my father's infusion, they would have fallen.

Jax's war hammer continued to ring as he fought the demon Abel and the exhaustion could be felt from the earth. And that is precisely when the earthquake started a low rumble in the land that tore the fabric open. Vines reached out, grabbing hold of demons, pulling them into the cracks and quickly closing, the reverberation of their screams and howls of despair the only evidence that they had been here.

Now the demons fled, those who could fly took off and the angels went after them. Aquarius and his host chased down those very same demons from above while the vines reached up to snag their prey. In what seemed like seconds, none were left except the two great battles in the sky.

I followed the fight between Abel and Jax, and just when it seemed Jax had finally gained the upper hand, Abel morphed into two beings. Cain lashed out and caught Jax's wing, toppling him towards Earth.

Iver raced for the sky and caught him, placing him gently

on the ground when he landed. Aquarius now took up the fight against Cain and Abel alone. Tabbris, Lucius, and Weigand Baidya took off to help their comrade.

Yemaya appeared at my side and gazed up at the sky. "Nice timing on the vines, Yemaya. Those nasty beasts didn't know what hit them."

She offered me a grim smile. "Thank you. I see Gula is already attending to Jax."

"Yes, hopefully, she can heal his wing quickly so he can get back in the fight."

She nodded her head, keeping her eyes on the battle in the sky.

"Look," Yemaya pointed, "it looks like Aquarius has taken out Cain. That just leaves Abel."

A roar rang out from the heavens that drew our eyes back to Finn, Isabelle and Michael. Isabelle was falling, her wings on fire. My breath caught as I watched my only daughter hurtling to her doom. Then, suddenly, she was suspended in the air. Gula was sending healing power, putting out the fire in her wings and restoring Isabelle's singed feathers, while my father held her aloft. Seconds felt like hours as we waited for Isabelle to open her eyes.

When she did, a cheer went up from our decimated army. Diana handed Isabelle her bow and arrows that had been dipped in Elysium. Isabelle found new strength and purpose, rose back to the heavens, knocked her bow, and let loose an arrow, piercing Michael in the shoulder. He let out a great roar and sped so quickly towards her that all my eyes saw was a streak of grey. Isabelle must have been anticipating his reaction and already had shot another arrow that found its mark. The archangel turned demon exploded, and all that remained were silver sparkles.

The sparkles seemed to take on a life of their own and accelerated into a circular pattern. The silver coalesced into a shape and finally stopped swirling. Michael was restored and back in angelic form. What could this mean? Our host was in shock as a giant hand reached out of the clouds, scooped Michael up, and disappeared. The same hand that had reached out for Isabelle in the lagoon?

And taking advantage of the shock, Isabelle drew her bow and let loose, hitting Abel right in his black heart. He managed to release one of his hell bombs before succumbing and blowing up into a million tiny stars. Isabelle lit up like a candle, encased in fire, screaming as she plummeted to Earth for the second time.

She's dead. My thoughts plagued me as I watched in horror. The angels sped after her, but none could touch her, or they too would be turned to flame. And that's when the most unexpected thing happened. My father, who had been garnering the last of his strength to save her, disappeared, and another appeared.

A young warrior rose into the air and captured the flaming Isabelle. At his touch, the flames rescinded and he floated to Earth with her safely tucked in his arms. Now I was running; I had to see if my daughter still lived. I arrived in time to see Weigand Beidya turn back to Iver and take his wife from the young warrior.

I didn't recognize him until he turned his eyes on me. They were my eyes, mine, and Isabelle's, our own unique shade of moss that only one other person had, Arkyn.

"But how, I don't understand?" Iver, too and all the immortals who stood close enough could see that Arkyn was no longer a child.

"It is as it was meant to be, Grandmother. The creature known as Azalthath is no longer. I contain his spirit, and as such, I am now the ruler of the void, and the heavens, the earth, the stars, and all things born out of the natural order."

"But, Arkyn, what does that mean, for us, for our only

son?" Iver held an unconscious Isabelle in his arms, but he had eyes only for his son.

Arkyn smiled, and as he did, the world was restored. The black gloom receded, Earth at once was filled with peace, birds sang, and the horrible battle was quickly becoming a distant memory.

"I will always be your son, Weigand Beidya, and I will visit, and you shall visit me. But no longer will I dwell in this realm. I am everything, all things, and my job now is to restore the heavens and Earth to their proper balance."

"And your mother?"

"She will awaken in time. Coming back from the dead comes with a cost, Father. But I promise you, she will be back to you soon."

"Deva?"

"She needs to spend time with Grandmother and me. Eons from now, this will be remembered as the war that brought the healing. Deva will one day replace Grandmother, and she still has much to learn. But I promise you, when Mother awakens, we will be there." And with that, Arkyn was gone.

Chapter 21

Jax

When a week after the battle, my sister still hadn't awoken, Finn and I went to work on convincing Iver to make our way to Scotland. Many of the immortals had stuck around to support Iver, who was a mess post-battle. Who could blame him? One event had changed his world forever. He missed his wife and his babies.

Finn and I missed our wives too, but we wouldn't leave him behind. When we finally convinced him that Issy would rather wake up in her own bed in her castle, basically, her favorite place on Earth, Iver made the decision to fly home.

Aleena had flown from New York to be with Lil and Vi. So Archer was with us, and it was a war-torn group of four that Serge picked up from the airport.

"It's true then, our Isabelle is in a deep sleep?"

Iver lifted her from the plane to the vehicle. "I have a lot to catch you up on, Serge. I know it's my first time home, and it's tradition to have a big festive welcome home feast with the staff, but I can't do it, at least not until Isabelle awakens."

"Besides," Finn cut in, "I have a goddess who needs my attention."

Serge patted him on the back. Those two had always been close, incredibly tight after Finn moved to Scotland.

Archer eyed me speculatively. "Me too. I take it my goddess is safely tucked away in a faraway corner of the castle so I can ravish her in privacy," he asked of Serge's retreating back.

"Yes, Archer, or is it Aquarius now?"

"Please, it's still me, little old, unassuming Archer, even though I am a god now." He flexed his arms, making all of us laugh.

"Seriously?" I punched him in the arm. "Now this is god power." I flexed my much larger biceps.

He laughed at me. "Yeah, well, when the muscle between your ears matches your arms, then we'll talk."

"Whatever, Archer, you're just jealous of my brawn," I said, getting into the vehicle. Archer and I continued to rub each other all the way to the castle. It was no secret that Archer and I had a bromance going on, and we were pretty tight.

"So," Serge spoke, "dare I ask what happened to our queen?"

The vehicle went quiet, waiting to see what Iver would say. When he kept quiet, Finn spoke up. "She was hit by a demon bomb, and she died for a moment. Then this incredible hero, who none of us knew, came and rescued her. It was Arkyn, older and looking more immortal if that's possible. He is the new God, by the way. Is it just me, or does that sound weird?" Not waiting for an answer, Finn continued. "Anyway, the slumber that Isabelle is in is required for rebirth or some such thing."

"Wow," Serge responded. "Sounds like I missed a lot."

"Yeah, like me kicking Abel's ass!"

"Oh, please," Finn cut in. "We both know you would have been dead in the first second if not for Isabelle."

"Yeah, Isabelle is the true hero, and she didn't even get to party afterward and have the rest of the immortals bowing at her feet."

"She never would have allowed that." Iver spoke up. "Isabelle would say it was a group effort, Jax."

He was right, and I felt a little embarrassed by my outburst, which was meant to be funny but fell short of the mark.

"He's right, though," Archer said. "Isabelle was glorious to watch in battle, wasn't she, Iver? I mean, talk about poetry in motion. I would say she has joined our ranks as one of the most skilled fighters in existence."

We all nodded our heads in agreement. "When we were fighting Michael," Finn added, "I felt like we were in some type of deadly dance, and the entire time she kept chanting, turning the tide of the war, right, Archer?"

"Yep, when she wakes up, Iver had better watch out, for his wife might be able to best him now."

Iver let out a low, sinister growl. Never screw with a hurting immortal who can morph into a wolf, I say. No one spoke another word until we were driving through the gates of Balmorton.

When we pulled up to the castle, I intended to head for home, but the ladies flew out the front door. Lil was positively glowing. I had never seen her look better. Pregnancy and focusing on her health had done wonders in the eight days I'd been gone. I pondered if I was too hard on her when I was around. The thought dissipated as she flung herself into my arms, dragging my face down to hers and planting a hungry kiss on my lips.

Our tongues danced as she wrapped her legs around my hips. My cock hardened beneath her ass, and the brat ground down as she sucked my tongue. When I was finally able to pull back, her pupils were dilated. "Goodbye, family. We'll see you tomorrow." I started to walk across the field to our house and remembered I could fly and be there much faster. I let out my wings to the laughter of those who remained behind. Let them have a laugh at my urgency. I needed some lovin' from my woman.

I flew up the stairs to our suite and landed on the bed. I quickly stripped and then did the same to my wife, and with an urgent need to copulate, I sunk my cock inside her waiting sheath. On the airplane to Africa, Lil had mentioned wanting to try having sex without gravity. As I took her hard, we lifted off the bed. Lil squeezed my hips with her thighs, her eyes rounded with shock.

She needed to get her mind off being airborne and on me. Out of nowhere, a hand came and spanked her ass. She squealed, looking around, but of course, no one was there. I performed the action with merely a thought. I spanked her again and added four more hands to pleasure her. Two to her lovely breasts, which were being tugged and twisted the way she liked it, while the other two gently massaged her. I gazed down at her saucily.

"Oh my goodness, holy crap, Jax, this is craziness!"

I was right when I said being weightless would be a game-changer. I grinned down at my sexy wife. "Yes, very true, but I'm far from done, Lil." I moved us until we were flipped around and facing the bed. This new vantage put Lil in a wheel barrel position, with her breasts hanging down and still being tormented to sweet perfection. She was squealing and begging, for what, she probably didn't know, as it was becoming evident that she was becoming lost in the multiple sensations she was experiencing.

My interpretation was she needed another cock buried inside her. So I added another slightly smaller version of mine to penetrate her ass, and as the cock slid in, Lil orgasmed fiercely, writhing in wanton abandon. Not giving her a chance to compose herself before lifting off again into orgasmic bliss, the spanking and anal penetration continued. But I pulled out of her and changed our position, our backs now facing the bed once more, and Lil, on a slight angle.

I added back the two hands to play with her nipples in time for Lil to unleash with a torrent of sounds that would make a porn queen blush. I spread her legs wide apart and watched as she writhed and bucked in what appeared to be one long, continual orgasm. I added two more hands to extend her arms and hold them in place while I moved around behind her head.

I slid my cock into her mouth. Now, all of her holes were full, while she continued to get lightly spanked, massaged, and her nipples pinched and tweaked. What a sight she made. Just watching the pleasure she was deriving, was enough to make me want to spill my load.

Lil softened her throat, and I slid farther inside and began fucking her throat too. It was like she was being taken by three of me at once, and her orgasms showed how turned on she was as wave after wave washed through her. Her mewls and primal screams reverberated off my hard rod, sending me to heaven. I pumped down her throat as I yelled with my release, which triggered another wave in my sexy wife.

Lil was a shuddering pile of goo by the time I finished with her and allowed her to float down to our massive bed. She lay as she landed, unable to move a single limb. "Jax, is there such a thing as being fucked to death because I think I came pretty close?"

I laughed and snuggled her into my side. "It would be a pretty good way to go, don't you think?"

She giggled lazily. "Yes, being fucked to death sounds

perfect. Except, I can't really die, and neither can you, so I guess I get this for the rest of my life."

"That you do. Now catch me up. What have you been doing since you got back?"

She batted her eyes, giving me her best innocent look. "Why, nothing, Daddy."

I laughed and sent her into the air above me.

"Jax! What are you doing?"

"You'll see." I moved my hand in the air as If I was patting something which transcended to her ass.

"Yikes! Ow, Jax, not fair!"

I paddled her behind a few more times with a paddle that wasn't really there and then watched her face as I played with her clit.

"Oh my god, no, not again, Ahh," she screamed.

I stopped playing and sunk a piece of ginger in her ass. I had to be careful that this new power didn't go to my head, because pleasuring her in all her orifices with my mind was quickly becoming my favorite candy.

Her face transformed, the paddle smacked her ass, she squeezed her cheeks, and the ginger trickled down to her little clit. She screeched and while I continued to torment her, I would sink this lesson home. She'd better behave because I could punish her any way I wanted.

"Please, please, please, I will be a good girl. Please take out the ginger."

I removed everything and again allowed her to float down to our bed. She snuggled into my chest. "That's some crazy shit, angel man."

I chuckled. "We're just getting started, baby."

Chapter 22

Lillith

We stayed in Scotland for another week before deciding that Iver needed Jax back at the helm. Or at least that was Jax's excuse. The thing is he loved work, and I took Gaea's advice in supporting this instead of fighting it. After all, our children would be running the worldwide empire one day, so it was best I get in line with it now.

Funny, being back and having more time to myself was not a burden like before our trip to Africa. I felt different somehow; renewed would be the best way to describe it, almost like I was given a do-over. When Jax told me about the battle and the hard-won victory, I realized that this new happiness was probably a direct result of our fight finally ending. With no more having to look over our shoulders for demons lurking in the dark, bent on our destruction, life had become almost idyllic.

With Jax's quick return to work, I decided to get busy in baby land. My first project would be the nursery. Observing and taking notes from Isabelle's nursery at Balmorton Castle had inspired ideas of my own. Instead of hiring a company to design the space, I decided to do it myself and contract out the work like Isabelle had.

I had just finished lining up the work to begin in two weeks when my phone pinged.

Violet: *Hiya, neighbor, whatcha doing?*

Me: *About to make a much-needed tea. You?*

Violet: *Would love to come over and join?*

Iver had purchased four matching penthouse apartments, ours and Finn's on our side, and across the street, two more. We could see each other clearly when we stood on our respective decks. I glanced out my window to Iver's empty deck and sighed. I really missed Isabelle and wished she could join us for tea.

Me: *Come, I would love to see you*

Less than a minute later, there was a knock on the door. "Come on in," I yelled. Violet dropped down on the opposite couch, looking frazzled. "Zara not sleeping? Why do you look so tired?"

Violet giggled. "I can't blame my daughter. It's her daddy. He's either playing with her or keeping me up all night by playing with me," she commented in an exasperated tone. But I knew better. Despite looking tired, her eyes danced with merriment. She was happy, and it looked good on her.

"Well, maybe he could play with her elsewhere and let you have a nap since you need more sleep than he does. I'm assuming, like Jax, since melding with his angel, he needs way less sleep?"

"Mhm, it's true. And Finn never gets tired, or bored, or stressed. Don't you find that strange?"

I pondered her question. "I think it's the new way of things. I mean, can't you feel the transition happening here, like Earth, here, I mean? Finn and Jax can focus on what they wish instead of keeping us safe all the time. It's a significant shift to move from survival mode into living."

Violet relaxed back into the couch and gazed outside as if the answers lay in wait outside my balcony doors. "I guess I hadn't stopped to think much. I've been so caught up in Zara and keeping up with my husband. So enough about that, how are the plans going for the nursery?"

My phone lit up with a call from the painters I'd hired. "Sorry, Vi, just let me get this, and then I'll answer your question." I took the call, only to find out that their contract dates had been bumped and they couldn't come for three months. I was hoping to be back in Scotland by then. But I agreed to the new dates and told them to keep me apprised of any other changes.

I closed my phone and sunk back into the couch, exasperated. "Speaking of the nursery... That was the painters; they've pushed the date out three months. Now I have to phone everyone back and change the other services dates and hope it is all done in proper order."

"No, you don't," Vi said excitedly. "Finn can do it, and while he's doing that, he can paint a fabulous mural on the walls."

"Yes!" I clapped my hands. "Do you think Finn will do it? I would so love that."

Violet didn't need to use her phone. She knew Finn would hear her talking to him. She closed her eyes, and like when Violet arrived, less than a minute later, Finn and Zara were at my door.

"Hey, sorry to bother you, but your wife volunteered you."

Finn and a gurgling Zara stepped in. "I don't know why you would bother hiring painters when you have such a talented brother-in-law living next door." Finn, Zara, and Vi followed me to the kitchen while I put on the kettle for tea.

"You know, Finn, that's a very good question. I guess

because Jax is at work every day, I just didn't think about it. But, now that you're here, can I show you the room and what I have in mind after our tea?"

"I'm here to make your dreams come to life." Finn laughed. "Of course, you can show me."

Once the tea was poured and Zara on her back cooing at the rattle in her adorable little hands, we discussed my plans.

"Have you thought about redecorating the nursery in Scotland, too?"

They didn't seem to have any ulterior motives in the question, but I felt that Isabelle's continued sleep was the elephant in the room and that they were really asking if I was going back to Scotland anytime soon.

"I am worried about Isabelle and Iver. I don't like us being so far away from them. I miss her dearly." I couldn't hold back the tears that leaked from my eyes. "I got to be part of Isabelle's journey. Our walks in the woods during her pregnancy and afterward, each of us carrying one of the twins on our backs... and I, well, I feel guilty for all of the joy I feel while poor Iver has no wife and no babies." Now I did cry, not for me, but for the loss of Isabelle's friendship and the pain Iver must be feeling.

Vi patted my hand. "I know how you feel. I'll never forget the first time I met Issy. She and Iver met us for lunch in Glasgow before the art opening, remember, Finn?" He responded with a smile. "I was so nervous. Iver was known as the king, and his pregnant wife was carrying the crown apparent. Isabelle was so powerful, even then, along with grace and acceptance. Both of them so kind and inviting, and all my nerves just evaporated. We had the best lunch, didn't we, Finn?"

Finn looked lost in the memory. "Thank you, my love. I have a vision for a new painting. I think I wish to immortalize that luncheon at the *'Ubiquitous Chip'* and give it to Iver and

Isabelle when she wakes up, and she will, Lil, don't fret. I'm guessing she will awaken before your babies are born."

"I'll hold you to that, Finn. Now, in answer to your question. I would love to get the nursery done in Scotland. I was thinking of making my way over there end of November. I love Scotland at Christmas. What do you say, you guys wanna come with and then you can do the nursery there too, if you don't mind, Finn?"

The couple exchanged looks before answering. "We'd love to. We were planning on attending a new art wing unveiling in December. Remember Lord and Lady Argyle? They were the wealthy benefactors who had the new wing built in the national museum and commissioned Finn to do some pieces? Well, the wing is ready, and Finn is one of the new featured artists representing Scotland, so we were planning on staying until the new year."

I started thinking. December first was eight weeks away, plenty of time to get things done and prepare for Scotland and Christmas. "I think your timing is perfect, a wonderful time to go. Aleena and Archer should join us too."

"Oh, and Raphe and Diana should meet us. It will be like the old days," Violet added.

"Well, then we have to add Luci, or he'll get jealous," Finn stated.

"I'm not sure." I giggled. "I hear that Luci has been with Diana's mother since the war. Maybe he'll be too busy to join us."

"Really?" Vi's eyes went wide. "That would be fun, wouldn't it?"

"Maybe we could go hunting for dinner." I giggled again, thoroughly enjoying this.

"Ladies, calm yourselves… Iver won't agree to anything if Isabelle has not wakened."

I thought about that. "No, it's still fine. I will host, as the manor home is plenty large enough to house twenty people. And my mother and Enoch will be coming anyway, and maybe Gaea and Centouri?" I aimed my comment at Finn.

"Yes, I had forgotten we had said we'd meet at Christmas. Also, I believe Freya will make an appearance."

"See, we have planning to do, and I would like to take the responsibility off Iver's household."

Finn chuckled. "Good luck not involving Claire. She would be quite put out if Christmas dinner isn't at the castle."

"Fine, then I will house the guests, and we will have dinner at Balmorton, but only if Iver agrees."

"Perfect, we have a plan, and with our precious Zara sleeping, let's go see that nursery," said Finn.

I jumped to my feet. "Right this way."

Chapter 23

Iver

When a week had passed since the battle and, still, Isabelle had not come back to me, itching to get home to their families, Jax and Finn finally convinced me to take my wife home to Scotland. I knew they were right, that she would want to wake up in her favorite place on Earth, but I wondered what the fallout would be when she found that her children weren't there to greet her.

I chose to believe my son, our new God, when he said he would be here when his mother awakened and clung to the hope that her awakening was inevitable. But as time passed, I was beginning to worry.

The brothers and Archer and their families had left about a week later, promising to be on the first flight back when Isabelle awoke. That was two months ago. We were almost at the end of November, and I'd had it. I needed my son to wake up my wife before I lost my ever-loving mind!

Breakfast was being served, but I wasn't paying attention, lost in thoughts of Isabelle. When I felt eyes watching me, I blinked several times up at Mrs. C, Claire, watching me intently.

"You need to eat, Iver. You're getting thin. What will Isabelle think when she wakes up and sees you like this?"

"It's time for a trip. I need to talk to Arkyn," I said, shoving a mouthful of waffles and sausage into my mouth and chewing like I was in a battle. Claire watched me until I asked, "What are you staring at? Seriously, have you not seen me eat before?"

"Not like that," she answered.

I stuffed another overly large portion into my mouth and muffled my response, "Like what?"

"Never mind. Now, what do you mean by *talk to Arkyn?* Can you just go and see him?"

Frustrated, I tossed my fork down on my plate. "I don't know! I am so done with this, Claire. I want my wife back, like yesterday!"

Claire offered me a sympathetic look. "I understand, but slow down, Iver. No matter how fast you eat, you won't fill the emptiness inside with food."

I pushed my plate away as the food in my belly turned to a hard lump. "You're right. I hate this, Claire. I have never felt more useless."

Claire sat down on the seat beside me and took my hand in hers. Long before Isabelle came into my life, Claire took care of the folks in my castle and me when I was in residence. When I'd met Isabelle, I hadn't been home in ten years. Since then, we'd made it our primary residence, and Claire, with the help of Isabelle's former guard, Serge, now Clarie's husband, had taken care of not only the castle, but the two hundred acres it sat on along with the village I supported.

"You are not useless. For the first time, you have folks you can really depend on to keep things going. Like Jax, and with the war over, you're not sure what to do with yourself is all.

Now, finish your breakfast, and go find your son. I will remain in the suite with Isabelle and alert you if her status changes."

I nodded in agreement, picking up my fork and finishing my breakfast and coffee. As I did, I thought back to when we left for Africa. So much had changed since we'd left Scotland, so much had changed since we'd come back... Isabelle missed the leaves changing color this year and one of her favorite fall activities, tromping through the woods beyond our pasture to witness the gorgeous array of autumn colors. Now it was gone, and sadness swept through me.

"Arkyn, son, please come to me and wake up your mother if you can hear me. I don't think I can survive another day without her."

I waited for a response, and when none came, I stood up from the table to leave for the veil. I was so lost in sorrow and memories, I almost missed the arrival of Arkyn. He, Deva and Gaea appeared, standing a few feet away. I shook my head to ensure my vision was real. I hadn't gotten to say goodbye to Deva, and the last time I saw her, she'd been a three-year-old child. Standing before me now, both my children couldn't be defined by age. They were ageless, like Gaea, and although they appeared to be around eighteen, their eyes held an ancient intelligence reminiscent of Azalthath, their grandfather.

"Father," Arkyn bowed his head respectfully, "Mother will awaken shortly, and we are here as promised."

I stepped the few feet separating me from my only son and pulled him in tightly to me. "I have missed you, Arkyn, so much." Then I added Deva to the group hug and was rewarded with her childish giggle I'd loved so much when she was little. Warmth imbued my heart and soul as I held my children for the first time in months. Over Arkyn's shoulder, I witnessed Gaea smiling at the happy reunion.

Arkyn pulled back. "Come, it is time."

"Welcome home," I said as we made our way up the staircase to Isabelle and my suite.

"I have been here, Father, with Grandmother, seeing to the healing of the land. Have you felt the shift?" Deva asked.

"I have been unable to feel anything good of late, my sweet girl. My heart has been heavy without my family."

"Poor Father," she said, taking my hand like she did when she was little. "I shall visit more often then, shall I?"

"Nothing would make me happier, little Deva."

We had arrived and moved through the sitting area to the bedroom. Every time I opened the door and saw Isabelle, I was reminded of the story of sleeping beauty. I'd met the true sleeping beauty, and in actuality, Isabelle looked nothing like Aurora. But with her calm expression and her hair fanned over the expansive pillow, there was definitely a resemblance. Aurora's tale had sprung up long after her death, but she had been considered beautiful at that time. Her story had been remembered and sung by minstrels for a thousand years before becoming a fairy tale.

Arkyn bid us stand on one side while he sat down on the opposite side of the bed. Taking his mother's hand in his, he said, "Mother, wake up now."

Isabelle's eyes fluttered open and regarded Arkyn. Her lips lifted into a Mona Lisa smile.

"Hello, Mother, welcome back from the land of sleep."

"I saw you in my dreams," she said with a bit of a croak from lack of use. "What happened? I feel I've been asleep for twenty years."

Arkyn smiled down at her with a love that was more than a son to his mother, a love that was encompassing, like a creator feels for his creation. He loved her being, and it was glorious to see. "Not quite, more like a few months. What do you remember?"

Isabelle's brow furrowed in concentration. "Not much."

Arkyn brushed his hand over her head. "How about now?"

"You brought me back from the dead." Her statement was filled with awe.

"I did. Father would have missed you too much, and we couldn't have the great Weigand Baidya be without his warrior queen."

She offered a small smile, but I could tell she was chewing on a disturbing thought. "You are the universe now, the one true God?"

"I prefer to think of myself as the scales that reset the balance."

Isabelle smiled and reached for his hand. "What of a mother's need to see her only son and daughter." She reached out her other hand out to Deva. "I shall miss you both terribly."

"We are always here, Mother, always in the fabric of your life and this plain. Deva has much work to do and will be on Earth for some time. She has already promised Father to visit more often. You will feel her presence acutely while she is here, even when her presence is not specifically in the castle."

Arkyn waved his hand over Isabelle and then pointed and twirled his finger in the air at me. "Father. Mother. Listen, and tell me what you hear."

Isabelle closed her eyes, and I followed her example. At first, I felt like a thousand tiny voices were calling from across a great distance. But as I listened harder, I realized I could separate them.

"That's right," Arkyn's voice said in my head. *"You are both now connected to my frequency. I will always be able to hear you, and you will always be able to hear my response. When you need me, I will come, and at Christmas, of course, I do need to stay connected to the first family."*

"The first family?" Both Isabelle's thoughts and mine mingled together in question. *"Yes, Earth's greatest king and his*

warrior queen, the great Wiegand Baidya and the Savior. You are my rulers here on earth, and I need to check in to ensure things are going as they should. In the days leading to the New Year, while a great transition is upon us, we will discuss the economy and new fuel sources, among many other topics."

Arkyn released Isabelle's hand and stood up from the bed. "I will see you soon," he said aloud.

The twins and Gaea were gone. Isabelle turned her tearful eyes to me. "I need you, Iver, please, come and hold me."

I climbed into the bed and pulled my wife close. It had been too long since our last embrace, and just feeling her alive and conscious, made my cock stand at attention. But now was not the time, now was the time to reconnect, I scolded myself.

"It has been too long since I felt you inside me," Isabelle said. Perhaps picking up on my internal battle?

"You are feeling fully restored?"

"I am and seem to recall you threatening to tie me to our bed to get your revenge."

"Later," I growled. "Now, I need to ravish every inch of you." I plunged my tongue into her mouth, cutting off her response. I missed her and couldn't get enough of her smell and taste. I kissed her neck and continued a trail of kisses down to her beautiful breasts, taking her puckered nipples into my mouth, one at a time.

"Mmm, that feels so good," Isabelle uttered, arching her back for more.

I wouldn't let her rush this. I wanted to worship her body, one I had been without for months now. I continued a trail of kisses down her belly, then lower, to the apex of her sex. She parted her legs, and I wrapped my arms around her thighs, pulling her sex to my mouth. I flicked my tongue, and Isabelle moaned. I licked up and down her seam and felt her body tensing with a building orgasm.

I purposely took my time licking and nipping before

plunging my tongue into her quivering channel. Her body spasmed with the invasion, and her walls tightened. I pulled my tongue out and laved her rear entrance, moving back to her clit and repeating the process several times. Isabelle was shaking, all her nerves firing at once as she unleashed her first orgasm.

As she released it in my mouth, my tongue was filled with her taste, igniting my hunger, and I could no longer hold back. I planted my fists down on either side of her ribs and thrust inside her.

Isabelle's eyes closed, submerging herself in the feel of my cock massaging her vaginal walls. I delivered long, hard strokes, and with each thrust, I felt her quivering and spasming, and it called to me, our bodies building towards a mutual climax.

"Iver," Isabelle panted beneath me, "I love you."

"I love you too." Playing with my new powers. I did a partial transformation, not becoming my full wolf, but my cock lengthened and thickened inside her.

Isabelle's eyes flew open with surprise. "Oh my goodness," she screamed as her chest flushed and she tipped off the edge into oblivion, and as she gripped my cock, I followed her off the cliff.

Chapter 24

Isabelle, the Savior

Iver only took breaks from making passionate love to me to text the gang and let them know I was awake. I desperately wanted to get out of the bed, as I'd been in one for so long, but Iver had other plans.

"I need to bathe you," he said after our third bout of lovemaking.

"I am feeling pretty dirty," I said, laughing. "But you have that effect on me."

He gazed down at me, pinning my wrists to the bed. "I have a bone to pick with you, wife."

I gulped. That wasn't my romantic Iver talking to his long-lost wife. It was alpha wolf Iver, talking to his mate. Answering appropriately, I simply said, "Yes, Sir."

Iver's gaze turned primal, and I watched in fascination as his canines elongated. Iver's voice deepened when he spoke next, his body growing and expanding before my eyes. "You were a very naughty girl, Isabelle."

The effect of his words sent a pang through my core, to my mound. How positively delicious, I'd play along. "Yes, Sir."

He growled, his eyes going dark. "Oh no, you don't," he said, his voice deep and guttural. "You have been naughty, and now Daddy Wolf is here to keep you in line."

Oh crap, this was so hot. I felt my cunt contract, releasing enough liquid to make the junction at my thighs wet.

Iver's nose lifted, sniffing my release, while I continued to watch him, fascinated by his partial transformation. "You like being in trouble, little girl." Not a question, but an observation.

Another contraction took me by surprise.

And now he let loose a chuckle that reminded me of a story about hell hounds I'd heard as a child. "You risked yourself, even after you promised to be safe. I have been in hell, waiting for you for almost three months. I told you before, I would tie you to my bed and not let you up until you learned that your place is at my side. But as your family is arriving tomorrow to celebrate, I will have to think of something else to teach you a lesson. I seem to recall your hate of being switched."

A convulsion swept through me as my body responded to him, even though he was right. I'd been switched once and hated it. Yet my body was betraying me, asking for the very thing I disliked.

He chuckled again in his deep, houndish voice. "I'm glad you remember, but unlike the first time, no hands required."

With that, I was suspended over an imaginary lap. I could feel Iver's thigh beneath my stomach, but he was still on the bed. Then I felt a tickling down my back, causing goosebumps to break out, and next, I heard the swoosh of a switch moving quickly through the air and felt the strike against my naked backside and the inevitable sting that followed.

I stared into Iver's piercing blue chips, while he watched

me getting my ass whipped. It was so hot, despite the pain, I couldn't help but be turned on. On the next lash, I screeched with the burning sting. Hands soothed my stinging backside while another set gently gripped my breasts. Iver continued to lord it over me while delivering numerous sensations to break me to his will. His mouth alternated, taking my nipples in his mouth. I had never had anyone play with my nipples while being spanked, and I found it intoxicating. The lash of the switch changed from being a tool of punishment into an instrument of arousal.

I was wet and could feel the slickness between my legs. Iver's increased wolf senses smelled my arousal. My legs were parted, and a finger flicked and teased my excited clit. "Oh, Iver, I'm going to—"

Everything stopped but the whipping, which picked up in intensity. "Oww," I howled in defiance. "What was that for?"

"Daddy, or Sir, you call me Iver again while we are playing out this punishment scene, and I won't allow you to orgasm, and trust me, I can leave you sexually frustrated for a long time." His eyes glinted menacingly, and I realized this wasn't a game to him. He was angry and exacting his revenge.

"Yes, Daddy," I answered obediently. Immediately, the intensity of the strokes softened to a tolerable level, and I let out a sigh of relief. This reminded me of the night I had asked him what to wear to dinner. The one and only time he'd had me call him Daddy. As I recalled, the dinner had been spectacular, and we'd had sex in the bathroom before we left the restaurant.

The switching suddenly stopped, thank heavens, and I hung limply over the invisible Iver leg, wondering what he would do to me next. Meanwhile, the real Iver had moved out of my range of vision. I heard drawers opening and closing. And then he was back in front of me and making a meal of my breasts.

While he was busy. I felt something probing my ass. A small plug? My answer came a moment later when my ass was fucked by the intrusive object and burned terribly. "Oh my god, ginger? You must hate me, Daddy!"

Iver chuckled as he roughly suckled each nipple in turn while I writhed and twitched, trying to dislodge the offending root. That's when the spanking started again, not a switch, but leather. Oh dear lord, not more heat! The leather seared the strokes made by the switch, and within a few lashes, my entire backside felt like it was on fire. I moaned pathetically, hoping Iver would take pity on me.

When I began to sob, he stopped. "Have you learned your lesson, little brat? You are mine. Never again, will you put your life before others. Swear it, and I will end your agony."

It seemed rather pointless to point out that we had been in a war and I just happened to be in the line of fire. I didn't put myself there. But Iver'd had a lot of time to replay the war and come to his own conclusion. So instead of arguing or denying what he said, I wholly submitted.

"Yes, Daddy, I was wrong. Please forgive me for not seeing the truth of my actions. I will never put my life before others again." That seemed to appease the beast. The ginger root was removed and the burn gone, my burning backside restored.

I was no longer being held up by an invisible knee but was being held by Iver, who'd shrunk back to himself. He held my eyes with his gaze, a mix of love and fear. "Never forget your promise, Isabelle. I can't live forever without you.

"I won't, I promise. I want to thank you, Iver."

"For what, my love?"

"You were right, from the beginning, when you asked me who protected me. Do you remember that night in the alley outside the club?"

Iver smiled. "I will never forget it or your response."

I giggled. "I thought I was pretty tough back then, that I had it all together. But I was so wrong. I was just young and ignorant, but you saw me, the real me, and I love you for it."

Iver's gaze shifted, the fear that had been there now completely gone. "I love you too, Isabelle. Now and forever."

He kissed me, and thoughts of the past or our unknown future fled my mind. I was with my forever king, and he was with the Savior.

Skylar West

Skylar West is a Canadian writer, new on the author scene and making a big impact with her steamy romance books. She loves walks in the rain, hot cups of delicious java, overly large sweaters, and the type of steamy sex she writes about in her novels. A cat lover, this author looks forward to writing many more novels.

Find her on Facebook: https://www.facebook.com/sky.west.1806

Don't miss these exciting titles by Skylar West and Blushing Books!

Sons of Sicily series
His to Learn
His to Train

Crown and Cross series
Laughlin
Malcolm

Angels and Demons Series
Fallen Angel
Dark Angel Discovered
Dark Angel Awakened
Dark Angel Rescued
Dark Angel Redeemed
The Savior

Single Titles
The Dark Side of Kingsley

Anthologies
12 Naughty Days of Christmas 2020